Devin Gazed Down At The Notes He'd Scribbled For Kerry Cottrell's File.

What he wanted to know was, was there a man in her life? No, he decided. No man worth his salt would let her walk away. It was obvious the lady wasn't taken.

He closed the file, thinking about what had happened in the past twelve hours. Something was definitely going on between them, something that would astonish Kerry if she knew. Something she probably wouldn't believe, even if he was fool enough to try to explain it.

Which he wasn't.

He didn't know what unknown quirk had linked the two of them. But he'd cope with that later. What he wanted to do right *now* would shock the lady right down to her pretty toes.

Devin grinned. Yeah, his plans for the delectable Miss Cottrell were definitely of *this* world....

Dear Reader,

When *Man of the Month* began back in 1989, no one knew it would become the reader favorite it is today. Sure, we thought we were on to a good thing. After all, one of the reasons we read romance is for the great heroes! But the program was a *phenomenal* success, and now, over six years later, we are celebrating our 75th *Man of the Month*—and that's something to be proud of.

The very first *Man of the Month* was *Reluctant Father* by Diana Palmer. So who better to write the 75th *Man of the Month* than this wonderful author? In addition, this terrific story, *That Burke Man,* is also part of her LONG, TALL TEXANS series—so it's doubly special.

There are also five more great Desire books this month: *Accidental Bride* by Jackie Merritt; *One Stubborn Cowboy* by Barbara McMahon; *The Pauper and the Pregnant Princess* by Nancy Martin—which begins her OPPOSITES ATTRACT series; *Bedazzled* by Rita Rainville; and *Texas Heat* by Barbara McCauley—which begins her HEARTS OF STONE series.

This March, Desire is certainly the place to be. Enjoy!

Lucia Macro,
Senior Editor

Please address questions and book requests to:
Silhouette Reader Service
U.S.: 3010 Walden Ave., P.O. Box 1325, Buffalo, NY 14269
Canadian: P.O. Box 609, Fort Erie, Ont. L2A 5X3

RITA RAINVILLE
BEDAZZLED

SILHOUETTE *Desire*®
Published by Silhouette Books
America's Publisher of Contemporary Romance

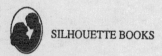 SILHOUETTE BOOKS

ISBN 0-373-05918-3

BEDAZZLED

Copyright © 1995 by Rita Rainville

RITA RAINVILLE

has been a favorite with romance readers since the publication of her first book, *Challenge the Devil*, in 1984. More recently, she won the Romance Writers of America Golden Medallion Award for *It Takes a Thief*. Rita was also part of the Silhouette Romance Homecoming Celebration as one of the authors featured in the "Month of Continuing Stars," and the Silhouette Romance Diamond Jubilee.

Rita has always been in love with books—especially romances. In fact, because reading has always been such an important part of her life, she has become a literacy volunteer and now teaches reading to those who have yet to discover the pleasure of a good book.

To all those who commit random acts of kindness
and senseless acts of beauty

Prologue

Devin Murphy jerked upright in the dark room, sweat trickling down his bare chest and back. Still grappling with tendrils of terror and panic, he was barely aware of the firm mattress beneath him, the sheet bunched at his hips.

He drew in a ragged breath—one part of his mind reacting to his pounding heart, the other part distantly reminded him the emotions he felt weren't his. They were part and parcel of his heritage, his telepathic link with his twin sister.

Megan.

The only person in the world whose feelings he picked up and reacted to as if they were his own.

What in the hell was she up to now? he wondered, punching the automatic dial button on the telephone next to the bed with an irritated jab of his finger. And why now? It hadn't happened in the last six months.

But he knew his sister well enough to know she couldn't stay out of trouble that long. Since the day she'd married Luke McCall—nothing.

He'd begun to think the link had been broken when—

"*What?*" a deep, distinctly annoyed voice snarled in his ear. "It's almost four in the morning. This better be good."

"Sorry," Devin muttered automatically. "I need to talk to Megan." In the taut silence that followed, he spared a thought for Luke's acceptance of the bond between the twins. It couldn't be easy being married to a woman who was psychically linked to another man—even if the man was her brother.

A soft, husky, feminine voice broke into his thoughts. "Hi."

"What's the matter?" Devin demanded.

"Not a thing, little brother. Not one little thing."

Devin blinked at the sound of her drowsy voice. It held no terror, no panic—just sheer contentment.

"Have you been out at Rainbow's End?" he asked, belatedly realizing that the recently remodeled bed and breakfast was the source of the fear he'd absorbed.

"Not for several days."

"Not tonight?" he persisted. "What were you doing just a few minutes ago?"

"Sleeping," she said pointedly.

Devin leaned back against the headboard, ignoring the cold teak against his damp skin. "Sorry, sis," he said finally. "I don't know what happened."

"A dream?" she asked softly, using the word that best described the knowing that frequently came during their sleep.

"Yeah, the usual. And since you're the only one I ever— Oh, hell," he said tiredly. "Go back to sleep. I'll talk to you later." He hung up, prodded his pillow and sprawled on his back, trying to convince his tense body that the alarm had been a wrong number. It was a hard sell because he didn't believe it, not for a second.

Megan didn't, either. She leaned across Luke, resting her head on her husband's hard chest. "That's interesting," she murmured, cradling the receiver. "Very interesting."

Luke's arm tightened around her waist. "What is?"

"Devin. Something weird is happening. He had a dream that upset him."

"What's so weird about that? You two do it all the time."

"Yeah, but this time it wasn't about me." She turned, crossing her arms on his chest and propping her chin on her wrists to gaze down at him. "I wonder if..."

"If what?" He waited patiently.

"If now that we're married, my bachelor brother has got himself linked to another woman."

Luke's eyes gleamed with amusement. "Does it work that way?"

"Not usually, but it did with our aunt Elly."

"Does he know that?"

Megan shrugged. "I don't know."

"Are you going to tell him?"

Megan chuckled. "Are you kidding? And spoil all his fun?"

One

"Wait a minute, let me see if I've got this right. You think I broke into this place and stopped to hang a picture before I made off with the silver?"

Devin stared at the woman asking the question, fighting both the adrenaline screaming through his body and a dazed sense of recognition. He knew her. He had never seen her before, but he knew her. He didn't recognize what was on the outside—although God only knew that was enough to stop any man in his tracks. No, he knew the intelligence and determination that energized her slim body, the deeply feminine spirit gleaming in her eyes. He knew it because he had spent most of his life searching for it.

She stood on a wooden chair, half facing him, the tip of one slim finger pressed to the wall. With her other hand, she smoothed a straying lock of brown hair behind her ear. A green pencil and a measuring tape laid on the hall floor at her feet. They had fallen when he'd stormed through the front door of the bed and breakfast with all the finesse of a bull elephant, gun drawn and ready to use. He had very nearly knocked her off her perch.

She hadn't screamed, hadn't panicked. Even now, she simply drew in a ragged breath, the only sign of her agitation. He gave her points for that—a lot of them, especially since he could see the frantic beat of her pulse in the hollow of her throat.

"Did I break a window, or was the door conveniently left open for me?" she added after a moment.

Most people wouldn't have heard the slight tremor in her husky alto voice, but then most people didn't have his training, Devin thought as she turned to face him more fully, still prodding the wall with the tip of her finger. Just as—luckily for them—most people weren't born into a family of psychics or with ESP.

So this is what they meant.

He had always considered it a quaint bit of family folklore, told by his father and a few older relatives. All male. One look, they said. That's all it took. One look at a particular woman, and they knew.

They hadn't told him it was like being kicked in the gut—or struck by lightning. What they *had* said was knowing didn't do them a damn bit of good, didn't make the chase any easier, because the woman never seemed to be struck with the same blast of intuition.

And now, watching this one shift restlessly beneath his steady gaze, he began to understand. Sensual hunger, instant and relentless, surged through him, prodding him to reach out and take what was his, while her only reaction seemed to be a growing uneasiness.

Devin blinked at the unfamiliar reaction. *His?* He wasn't a possessive man. He considered himself a liberated male, accepting women in the modern work force, encouraging them to stretch and grow. He had too many female relatives to feel otherwise. He had never been an advocate of the barefoot-and-pregnant school of thought.

So why was he looking at this woman and getting some very primitive ideas?

"Did I leave a trail of bodies behind? Or—"

Devin raised his hand in a peaceful gesture, hoping that he *wasn't* dealing with a sensitive woman. The last thing he needed at this point was for her to read his mind. "Okay. I was wrong. I'm sorry. Really," he added at the skeptical lift of her brows. "I don't usually barge in like this, but when I saw the open door—"

"You thought I was a thief." She gave an understanding nod. "Makes sense. If you're the suspicious type."

He didn't bother to tell her he was. She already knew. "I didn't think anyone was here. Anyone legal, that is."

"That's okay. I came a week early," she murmured absently, glancing down at the floor. "Would you hand me that pencil, please?" She took it from him and carefully removed her finger and made a mark on the wall. "Great. Thanks. I didn't want to have to measure that again. Pictures are a royal pain to get straight."

Great? *Thanks?*

Well, at least she wasn't the hysterical type, he reflected, his gaze fixed on the slender fingers clenching the pencil. He had scared her. Hell, he'd done more than that, he'd terrified her. But was she going to show it?

No.

A gutsy lady, he decided, taking in her determined effort to steady her breathing. She was staying in a house in the middle of nowhere, furnished with—he took another look around—exactly one picture and a chair, and she was willing to take him on. Yeah, real gutsy.

Even when he'd shoved his gun into the holster at the small of his back, she hadn't blinked. The pencil and tape had slipped from her fingers, but she hadn't dropped the hammer. It was now swinging gently from her small, tight fist.

So what he had here was a small, frightened woman who would die before she'd admit it. She might turn purple from lack of oxygen, but he knew she'd come up with a damn good reason why she wasn't breathing on a regular basis. He grinned at the back of her head. There was pride in the tilt of that pointed chin, lots of it. And stubbornness. Lots of that, too.

Hopping down, she placed the hammer on the chair and turned to him, extending her hand. "You have to be my boss's brother, head of security for Luke McCall's interests on the island. The red hair and blue eyes gave you away. As well as the gun," she added dryly. "I'm Kerry Cottrell."

Something in his steady gaze made her uneasy again. Nodding to the painting propped against the wall, she said brightly, "Your sister left this to welcome me. I decided to hang it as my first official duty."

Devin knew the picture well. Luke had commissioned the painting as a gift for Megan. It was the original plantation house—a large, rambling structure that looked much like a huge grass shack with deep eaves, large windows and a wraparound porch. A dazzling rainbow began at the horizon behind the trees and appeared to end in the center of the roof. At the bottom, an engraved brass plate said Rainbow's End.

Ignoring the picture, Devin took Kerry's small hand in his. "You're right, I'm Devin Murphy. I gather you're the new manager?"

She nodded. "And before you even think it, let me assure you—I'm neither as young nor as naive as I look."

She couldn't be. Neither his sister nor brother-in-law would turn over their new baby to anything less than a paragon. Devin reluctantly relinquished her hand.

"I think it's my eyes," she said thoughtfully, turning them up for his inspection.

She had a point. They were green, flecked with gold and turquoise, extravagantly lashed and slightly tilted at the corners. If they had been brown, they could have belonged to Bambi. A quick glance gave the impression of vulnerability and innocence that probably misled a number of people, he reflected. A closer look revealed the intelligence gleaming in those hazel eyes, as well as a measuring assessment that clearly stated Kerry Cottrell was no fool. A hint of mischief overrode the entire effect.

He figured she knew those things about herself. He wasn't so sure if she was aware of the feminine passion lurking among the green and gold and turquoise.

Her hair was light brown shot through with highlights of red and gold, the silky mass fighting the restraint of the precarious knot coiled atop her head—

and winning. Tendrils were drifting down, kissing her nape, touching her shoulders.

There was nothing provocative about the modest blue shorts and baggy T-shirt that covered her slender curves, nothing to make his body clench with desire. Nothing to make him picture her between the sheets of his large bed, her long, slim legs wrapped around him.

Nothing at all.

Kerry took another deep breath, hoping it didn't sound as shaky as it felt. It wasn't just his John Wayne, hell-for-leather entrance that bothered her. It wasn't even the gun—which she disapproved of on general principles and thoroughly disliked. No, it was more than that.

It was . . . *him*.

She had been expecting a masculine version of his blue-eyed, half-Hawaiian, half-Irish elfish sister, Megan. Someone who would be right at home in Santa's workshop.

Smothering a small sigh, she wondered gloomily if she would ever learn to gauge a man correctly. Any man. After a few seconds' thought, she decided if the last year was any indication, probably not. It had been . . . confusing. Unpleasant. And taking into consideration the fact that she'd expected to have a handle on this male-female thing by the time she was twenty-seven, it was also discouraging.

Charles, a man she had dated on occasion, had misread her warm offer of friendship for something infinitely hotter—a condition that seemed to be happening with alarming frequency. He had been her next-to-last mistake. Jared had been the final straw. Not only had he reached the same conclusion as Charles, he'd driven her to distraction with his mule-headed insistence that they were soulmates. His psychic, he'd assured her earnestly, had told him so.

Kerry sighed again as she looked at Devin. This was no sprite, no elf, no good-natured leprechaun. No harmless male who would slip comfortably into the role of friend and companion.

On the contrary.

He was a moviemaker's dream. If casting directors had been scouring the islands for a man who could simultaneously stare down a gunslinger, whip a roomful of thugs and dazzle a woman with just a smile, Devin Murphy would have had them turning cartwheels.

But she was made of sterner stuff, Kerry reminded herself. Experience—especially the negative kind—was a great teacher. Besides, she wasn't looking for a man. They simply weren't in her short- or long-term projections. Not these days. Especially not an intimidating, larger-than-life type like Devin.

The situation with Charles and Jared, both of whom had seemed like pleasant, ordinary men, had resulted in a jarring insight—she was apparently a rotten judge of men. Both incidents—they had definitely not progressed to affairs—had ended with ruffled feelings all around and convinced her to put her social life on hold while she concentrated on her career.

A job made in heaven had reinforced the decision. It had promised travel, adventure and escape from Jared's idiotic fixation with psychic soulmates. If the man had been open to rational discussion on the topic, she reflected, he'd have seen the flaw in his argument. He couldn't possibly be bound through eternity to someone who viewed the entire subject of psychic phenomena with open skepticism.

"So you came here early?" Devin prompted.

Kerry blinked away the past and concentrated on her boss's brother. First impressions, she reminded herself. "Uh-huh. I gave myself a three-week vacation on the islands but called it off after two."

"Why?"

She shrugged. "Several reasons."

"What was the most important one?"

Moving the hammer and perching on the edge of the chair, Kerry frowned up at him, forgetting about impressions—first or any other kind. "Are you always this pushy?"

"Yep." He nodded. "Some people call it an occupational hazard. I call it honing my skills. So, why did you cut your vacation short?"

Giving a sharp sigh, she snapped, "Because someone broke into my hotel room and I didn't feel safe. I wanted to come to my own place." For all the good that had done, she thought moodily. She had tossed and turned all night.

In the clear light of day, she was willing to write off the restless night as imagination. The sounds she'd heard had obviously just been normal house noises. Her first night in a new place was always an uneasy one.

"Were you hurt?" Devin's voice was hard.

"In the robbery?" She shook her head. "No. The burglars had come and gone before I got back to my room."

"What did they take?"

"That's the crazy part of it. Everything was in a mess, but I couldn't find anything missing. The hotel security people speculated that the thieves were scared off by a noise." She shrugged. "The telephone or maybe voices in the next room."

He frowned and said slowly, "Or maybe they didn't find what they were looking for."

"So they followed me here and are waiting in the bushes until they can try again? That's a comforting idea. Thank you very much." Kerry gave him a cross look. "More than likely, they just didn't find anything worth taking. There was no money or jewelry in the room, and I had my camera with me."

"There are other things thieves look for."

"Like what?"

Devin shrugged. "Documents, microfilm."

Her eyes widened. *"Microfilm?* I'm not a spy, for heaven's sake! Or a blackmailer. Or anything else. Look, Mr. Murphy—"

"Devin."

She gave an exasperated sigh. "Devin. You obviously have no idea what an ordinary life I live. The only information in my room was a list of tourist spots I was going to hit the next day. In terms of value, it wasn't worth the paper it was written on."

"How'd you sleep last night?" Devin asked, propping a shoulder against the wall and watching the changing emotions on her expressive face.

"Fine, just fine."

Devin sighed at her too-quick response. "Don't ever take a job that requires you to lie."

"I know." Kerry scowled. "I'm rotten at it. But I'm not a child, and I don't need a nursemaid."

His grim look lightened. "I couldn't agree more." He waited a beat. "So, how much sleep did you get?"

She leaned forward in the chair, her elbows on her thighs, watching the hammer as it swung in a small arc between her legs. "Very little," she admitted finally. "I kept hearing creaks and imagining that someone was trying to break in here, too."

Devin closed his eyes for a second, fighting the growing suspicion that he knew exactly when she had reacted to the noises. And how often. "Are you going to feel safe out here?" he asked abruptly.

"Don't be silly. Of course I am."

Again, her reply came too quickly for his peace of mind. He didn't know if she was trying to convince herself or him, but if the apprehensive look she cast around the large, empty hallway was any indication, she failed miserably—on both counts.

"I don't like it," Devin told her slowly, his gaze following hers, stopping at the bare windows.

"Don't like what?"

"You being out here by yourself. The place isn't even furnished."

"The phone's in," she said hastily. "And I have water and lights. Besides, it won't be empty for long. Megan told me that she and Luke have a warehouse full of stuff. They'll start delivering now that I'm here."

"That doesn't change the fact that your nearest neighbor is three miles away." His voice was flat. "Or that at night, anyone could look through the windows and see that you're here alone."

"But—"

He held up a hand, stopping her. "Contrary to the chamber of commerce hype, this isn't always a paradise. There are a few snakes crawling around." He ran a hand through his hair and swore softly. "Hell, they haven't even installed the wiring yet. It's scheduled for this week."

Kerry looked at the lazily drifting overhead fan. "But—"

"I'm talking about the security system." He watched moodily as the hammer swung over bare toes covered only by a couple of narrow bands of leather.

"Wiring?" She gave him a worried frown. "That sounds messy. I'm going to have rugs and furniture delivered, remember?"

"They'll have to do some drilling." He shrugged. "It can get dirty. Look, why don't you stay at a hotel in town this week while my crew comes out here? McCalls will pick up the tab. Take that extra week of vacation. When we're done, you can come back and get to work."

Her stubborn resistance was as clear as a shout, and just as loud. He registered it even before she began shaking her head. Devin pushed away from the wall and moved to the open door, looking out over the wide, planked porch, thinking of his own sleepless night, of his aunt Elly.

The family grapevine had worked overtime when Elly had reported in shortly after her twin's wedding. She was picking up messages, she said in bewilderment, and they weren't coming from her brother. It had taken her a few weeks to locate the source of havoc, and several more to deal with the seesawing emotions of the man involved—a stuntman who was terrified of a pending skydiving scene. The family members had watched the events closely—all the way to her eventual marriage with the stuntman—having a vested interest since almost all of them had, to some extent, psychic ability. If it happened to Aunt Elly, they reasoned, it could happen to them.

But this thing with Kerry isn't the same, he assured himself, turning to watch her gear up for the argument. Setting aside his blatant sexual response to her, whatever he was picking up from her was simply a result of her expressive face and his ability to read body language. It had nothing at all to do with telepathy. He wasn't linked with her. Absolutely not.

Definitely.

Period.

Devin turned toward her just as the swinging hammer slipped through her fingers and dropped like a stone on her bare left foot.

"Ouch!" Kerry drew her injured foot to her opposite knee, cradling it in her hands. "Talk about stupid," she muttered between clenched teeth. "I don't believe this."

"I don't, either," Devin muttered as pain, sharp and unforgiving, pierced his left instep and blossomed, radiating to his toes and ankle.

"Damn it, Megan, it's not funny." Devin got up from behind his desk, his fingers tightening around the receiver.

"I'm sorry." Her voice drifted through the telephone, husky with mirth. "Tell me again."

"What's to tell?" he exploded. "Less than four hours ago, your new manager dropped a hammer on her foot and mine felt like it damn near fell off."

"Did hers hurt?"

"Of course it did." He scowled at the etched glass of his office door, reading the backward gold letters that said Private Investigations. "You know as well as I do whose pain I was feeling."

"Fascinating, isn't it?" she asked brightly. "Uh, Devin?"

"Yeah?"

"Do you remember Aunt Elly?"

"She's all I've been thinking about since I woke you up last night."

"Do you..."

"No." The short word cut off her hesitant pause. "Don't even think it."

"I wouldn't dream of it. Devin?"

"Now what?"

"I don't like the idea of Kerry being out there by herself with no security system."

"I don't, either, and I told her so."

"What'd she say?"

He scowled. "That I didn't have to like it. She was fine, thank you very much, and to butt out."

"She said that?"

"A little more politely, but that was the gist of it."

Megan chuckled. "And what did you say?"

"That I'd be spending the nights out there until everything was installed."

"And?"

"She was thrilled," he said dryly. The husky sound of Megan's laughter made him grin.

"I'll bet she was."

His smile faded. "Thrilled or not, I'll be there, and she knows it. Meg, are you sure Kerry can run the place? She looks like—"

"I know." Megan's voice was resigned. "A kid."

"No." His voice was even. "That's not what I meant. She just looks so..." He stopped, realizing he didn't know what he meant. Not naive. Not exactly. Not gullible. So what was it?

"Not to worry," Megan soothed. "You'll figure it out someday. In the meantime, rest assured. When Luke had to go to San Francisco on business, I went along to interview her. She was managing a B and B outside the city, and I stayed there a night as a guest.

"She's incredible, Dev. Ran the place like clockwork, and she's wonderful with the guests. The office was a model of efficiency. Believe me, we're lucky to have her. In fact, I heard through the grapevine that the owners offered her a great package—more than we're paying her—to stay another year until they could retire and take over themselves. Frankly, I don't know why she didn't take them up on it, but I'm not about to rock the boat by asking."

"Want me to find out?" Devin lounged against the corner of his desk, a smile turning up the corners of his mouth. "I'm a hotshot detective, remember?"

"Devin!" Megan's voice was alarmed. "Don't you dare do anything to upset her. When Luke bought the three plantations, I promised him I'd get them all restored within two years. I can't do it if you chase off our manager, so behave!"

"You wound me."

"I'll do more than that if you mess things up! I mean it, Devin—"

He hung up on his sister's sputtering, gazing down at the notes he had scribbled while talking to her. They were for Kerry's personnel file—an otherwise empty file since she had been hired before he'd agreed to run security checks on all McCall Enterprises' island employees.

Actually, he realized, he wasn't worried about her professional qualifications. He had a feeling that she could handle anything she tackled. She had the look of a lady who set her goals high—then exceeded them.

What he wanted to know about was her personal life. Was there a man? He gazed at the near-empty file and shook his head. No. There wasn't. At least not one to worry about. No man worth his salt would let her walk away for a job. More importantly, she didn't act committed. No, it was obvious the lady wasn't taken, and she definitely wasn't looking.

Devin closed the file, his thumb brushing the glossy surface of the folder as he considered the past twelve hours. Something was definitely going on between them, something that would astonish Kerry if she knew. Something she probably wouldn't believe, even if he were fool enough to try to explain it.

Which he wasn't.

He still didn't know for sure if an unknown quirk of fate had linked the two of them on some astral plane. He supposed it had, he reflected moodily, flexing his sore foot. But he'd cope with that later. What he wanted to do right now would shock his sister's manager right down to her pretty toes.

Devin's grin was full of anticipation. Yeah, his plans for the delectable Miss Cottrell were very much of this world.

Two

"You're back. I didn't think you really meant it."

Kerry, sitting on the top step of the porch and waiting for what promised to be a spectacular sunset, frowned at Devin when he slammed the door of his black Blazer and headed toward her.

He dropped a small duffel bag on the bottom stair, eased down beside her and shot a quick glance at her profile. "You knew I did."

"One can hope," she muttered, determined not to show him how relieved she was. Somehow the house seemed much larger, much emptier and more isolated in the dark. And yes, she had believed him, but there was a credibility factor here, she reminded herself. If the McCalls thought she needed a keeper, how much confidence would they have in her as a manager?

Zippo.

"I assume you brought a sleeping bag?" She got a small flare of satisfaction from his wince. "And maybe a foam pad? The floors are pretty hard."

"Terrific. That's just what I need to top off a perfect day."

Kerry watched in silence, trying to enjoy the hush of the balmy April evening as the sun dipped behind the line of trees in a blaze of scarlet and gold.

It wasn't easy.

Sitting next to Devin was like getting cozy with a time bomb. She had felt his simmering intensity as well as his massive control when, gun drawn, he'd burst through the door. Focused, ready for anything, he'd reminded her of a lethal cat poised to strike. He'd scared the daylights out of her.

She didn't feel noticeably better now, she thought wryly. Even relaxed—claws retracted, so to speak—he was still a force to reckon with. The energy was controlled, tamped way down, but it was still there.

He wasn't handsome, even with blazing blue eyes and auburn hair that gleamed like dark fire. There was simply too much power and determination in his lean face for it to be considered good-looking. But he would do, she thought uneasily as she edged a few inches away.

He obviously wasn't the type to spend much time in front of a mirror, Kerry decided after a few moments of reflection. With no beard or mustache to trim and a no-nonsense, conservative cut that controlled the wave in his thick hair, it probably took him a flat two minutes to get ready in the morning.

And his mouth, she thought, closing her eyes for an instant. Oh, his mouth. Well-shaped lips that curved in the barest hint of a smile made a woman wonder if they felt as good as they looked.

Yes, indeedy, she thought with a sigh, he would certainly do.

Staring determinedly at the early blooms on the big poinciana tree, she resolutely turned her attention to the yard. Actually, it was three acres of land that surrounded the house and separate cottages, resembling an arboretum. Dotted with towering trees and flowering shrubs from around the world, the place would be a showpiece when Mr. Kimura and his merry band of gardeners were finished. As far as she was concerned, it already was. She turned her head, gazing thoughtfully at a majestic banyan tree, and wondered if any of the pictures she'd taken that morning would reflect its ancient grace.

When the last of the color faded from the sky, Kerry turned to face Devin, her mood momentarily softened. "I've only been here a day and I'm already in love with the place. When the tourists discover it, they'll be fighting for rooms."

He nodded. "That's what Megan said right from the beginning. When everyone else saw a tumbled-down plantation, she saw the potential."

"What about Luke? Surely he had the same vision."

Devin grinned. "He didn't have a clue. He bought this place and two others strictly for the locations, with plans to build something that would fit the McCall image."

"You mean something that would match his hotels?" she asked in horror. "Not that they aren't nice," she added hastily, "but they're nothing like this."

Devin shrugged. "I think that was the idea. Then he heard about a local miracle worker—Megan—who had done some great work on several old places. He went after her, but her reaction was the same as yours. She wanted the job so bad she could taste it, but she would only agree to work on it if she could do it her way."

"And how was that?"

His gesture took in the house behind them. "To get rid of the clutter some of the later residents had tacked on the house and go back to the island style of the original builder. Our Megan's big on keeping the past alive," he added, affection for his sister evident in the warmth of his voice. "And that's why you have what looks like an overgrown grass shack built with New England know-how and ingenuity."

"It's beautiful!" Kerry protested.

"I didn't say it wasn't. All I meant was that many of the old homes aren't. Most of the missionaries and early settlers weren't smart enough to adjust to the climate. They built carbon copies of their homes in New England, with high ceilings and small windows."

"And suffered for their tunnel vision, no doubt."

"Exactly. They sweltered. The guy who built this place took the best from both worlds. He made sure the construction was solid and put large windows on all four sides for cross ventilation."

"Clever," she murmured.

"Mmm."

She eyed him curiously. "It's not?"

"It's hell on security."

"Oh."

"Yeah, 'oh.' And since I oversee that end of things, I'm stuck with it."

He was tired, she realized abruptly, and he did look as if he'd had a rough day. He had probably been out chasing bad guys, she thought hazily, or whatever it was private investigators did, and now, when he would normally be at home relaxing, he was here to make sure she got through the night safely.

Fatigue should have softened him somehow, she reflected, giving him a quick sideways glance. Gentled his granite profile or something.

It hadn't.

It should at least make him look less dangerous.

It didn't.

She doubted that anything less than a coma would manage that. But hard or soft, dangerous or not, he was tired. He was also trying to protect her—whether she needed it or not—and she was telling him he had nothing more than a hard floor to sleep on. The very idea was enough to have her hospitable ancestors spinning in their graves.

Kerry got up and tugged at his shirtsleeve. "Come on, I have a surprise for you." She led him inside to a large room at the back. *"Voilà."* With a flourish, she threw open the door and gestured toward the massive bed and dresser planted solidly against the far wall. Before he could ask, she said, "I talked with Megan this afternoon and got some of the basics cleared up. I'm to take the suite upstairs, and this is yours for as long as you need it. Apparently you have a cousin who rents furniture?"

Devin nodded. "Pete."

"And another one who owns a bath and bed shop?"

"Laura."

"And one with a grocery store?"

"Art."

"Does your family populate the entire island?" she asked politely.

Devin grinned. "Almost."

"Well, I made a few calls, said the magic words— Megan McCall—and now we have beds, sheets, towels, soap, toothpaste, a coffeemaker and some food, as well as a kitchen table and chairs. They even delivered," she added in an awed tone. "I *know* I'm going to like this place."

And now she would thank him, she decided. At least she would as soon as she figured out how—without sounding like a total idiot. A dependent idiot. Moving her gaze up to look over his broad shoulder, she realized with a jolt just how big Devin Murphy was. He topped six feet by two or three inches, and her by eight or nine. And every one of those inches was packed with lean, lethal power.

Since they had parted earlier, he had changed his clothes—if not the style. He wore a colorful Hawaiian shirt, faded jeans that clung to his lean hips and muscular thighs, and running shoes. He looked just as competent as he had that morning. She wondered if he still had a gun tucked in his waistband.

Probably.

Kerry frowned, for the first time giving the matter some serious thought. What on earth kind of job was this? Her previous employment, described in glowing detail on her fancy résumé, had covered a broad spectrum, but she had never worked where a gunslinger was required to stand guard.

Shrugging, she put the question on hold and returned to the issue at hand. Just say it and get it over with, she lectured silently. Then you can go to bed with a clear conscience and catch up on lost sleep.

"Uh, Devin?"

He took his gaze off the bed and turned it toward her. "Yeah?"

"I just wanted to..." She cleared her throat and started again. "I'm glad you're going to be here tonight."

Eyeing her thoughtfully, he asked, "Is that so hard to admit?"

"Yes, damn it, it is." She frowned up at him. "Because I feel like a fool. Being alone in an empty house has never made me nervous before. I'm not the type who needs her hand held once the sun sets. I've been on my own for a long time, and I manage very nicely. I don't want Megan or Luke to think I'm not—"

"Relax. Your protest is duly noted—and quite unnecessary." He rested his large hands on her shoulders, tightened his fingers fractionally, then moved her aside, walking back the way they had come. He went systematically through the house, checking the locks on the windows in each room, trying to concentrate on the job at hand rather than the hazel-eyed distraction following him.

"What do you mean—unnecessary?" Kerry asked, trotting along behind him. The man was thorough, she noted idly. Annoying, more than a tad unpredictable, but thorough. She had to give him that.

"I mean, I'm not here because any of us thinks you can't do the job," he told her, tugging on a closed window and giving a satisfied grunt when it didn't shift.

"Then why—"

He held up his hand, stopping her. "Because this place is isolated, and you got here before the alarm system did. End of story, end of discussion."

"You really are an annoying man," she said, frowning at him.

Devin grinned. "Better to have you mad than scared."

"I'm *not*—"

He gave her a thoughtful glance. "Then maybe you should be."

"Don't even start with that stuff." Her hazel eyes snapping with irritation, she said distinctly, "There's no one trying to get in the house, and there's no one following me. I don't spend my life seeing bad guys around every corner the way some people do."

They had circled the lower floor and were back at the central staircase. Kerry rested a hand on the broad oak banister, narrowing her eyes.

"All I need is a good night's sleep and I'll be fine," she told him contrarily. "Just fine. So I'll say goodnight. See you in the morning."

Devin waited until she was halfway up the staircase. "Kerry?"

She stopped, her hand still on the wooden rail. Looking down at him, she drew in a quick breath. His blue eyes were bright with masculine appreciation and something more lethal that she didn't want to acknowledge, much less analyze.

"What?"

"I'm going to do a quick check around the outside, then do the same upstairs. So if you hear anything, it'll be me."

"Okay." She waited a few seconds, and when he just stood there, calmly watching her, she raised her hand in an agitated gesture and muttered another hasty good-night.

Kerry closed the bedroom door behind her and leaned against it with a ragged sigh. The room wasn't truly a refuge, but it offered a measure of privacy. And peace. Especially while a rock-hard man was prowling around the rest of the house.

He made her nervous.

She considered the revelation as she headed for the bathroom and her toothbrush. It wasn't her nature to be intimidated by people—even very large men. But in this case, she would reluctantly make an exception. According to Megan, her brother was good with a gun and better in hand-to-hand combat. He probably ran marathons in his spare time, Kerry thought as she brushed her teeth vigorously. He definitely wasn't the typical guy next door.

But it wasn't fear she was feeling, Kerry silently admitted. Despite his height and strength, despite his warrior abilities, Devin Murphy would never harm her. No, it was her instinctive response to his blatant masculinity that was setting off alarms. He touched something within her, down deep where it counted. He set off a thrumming awareness in her blood that every feminine cell in her body responded to. Her mind drifted to Charles and Jared as she reached for a towel. As annoying as they had been, they hadn't considered artillery part of their wardrobe. Now that she thought about it, maybe they hadn't been that—

"Kerry!"

Devin's voice on the other side of the door scattered both her thoughts and the towel. Before she could gather either, the door flew open.

"Have you ever heard of knocking?" Her scowl was as fierce as his as she marched to the door, her fists planted on her hips. "What do you want? *What?*"

"Did you do anything to the windows downstairs?"

She glared at him, momentarily speechless. "You break in here like a maniac—"

"Don't exaggerate. Just tell me if—"

"To ask me if I did anything to the—"

"You touched the damn—"

"Windows?"

"Windows!"

Kerry took a ragged breath. He'd stand there until he turned to stone, she decided in disgust after studying his determined expression. Or at least until he got an answer. She thought briefly of letting him wait, then decided she'd rather cooperate and up the chances of getting to bed before dawn.

"Yes," she said evenly, "I certainly did do something to them. I washed them. Each and every one of them."

"Outside?"

She sighed. "No. I'm calling a commercial cleaner to do the outside. Why?"

"Because someone tried to jimmy two of the dining room windows."

"Jim—" She stopped and shook her head. "No. It doesn't make sense. There's nothing in here a thief would want. More to the point, there's nothing to take. Even an incredibly stupid burglar would figure that out. No, it must have been an animal."

"Sure. One that tried to gnaw the windows open?"

Kerry shrugged. "I don't know. What kind of animals do you have around here?"

"None that break into houses. At least, none with four legs."

Kerry tapped her foot impatiently. "This whole thing is crazy. Why would anyone even bother? I want to see those windows."

"Why?"

She narrowed her eyes in irritation. "Because I'm the manager, that's why."

He leaned a shoulder against the doorjamb, watching the expressions reflected in her vivid face. Annoyance, impatience, outright anger, but no fear. She might admit to a bit of nervousness, but he had a feeling that when the chips were down, not much fazed Kerry.

"You're not on duty yet," he reminded her blandly. "You got here a week early, remember? Officially, I'm still in charge."

"I just changed the rules," she informed him, attempting to get by him. "I'm here, I'm the manager, and it's my problem. Will you *move?*"

Devin stepped back and led the way out the front door and around the house. When he stopped, she rushed ahead, so he scooped her against him and held her there. "Watch the footprints," he warned, shining his flashlight on them. "I want to check them out in the morning."

Kerry obediently glanced down at the clear impressions in the soft soil. They were large, with the crisscrossed tread of running shoes. Next, she examined the shredded wood on the sill. "Are you sure the carpenters didn't leave it that way?'' she asked hopefully.

"Not a chance, sweetheart. I've checked this place too many times since they finished. The last time was when I made a swing around here yesterday. And,'' he added disgustedly, "I should have checked it this morning while I was here."

Taking advantage of his loosened embrace, Kerry slipped away and stepped over to the next window. It was in the same condition.

"Why do you suppose they stopped?" She reached out to run a finger on the section of the gouged wood and shivered.

Devin caught her wrist before she touched it. "Watch it, there's a chance they left some prints. As for stopping, who knows? Maybe they didn't know how to use the jimmy, and if that's the case, they better take up another profession." His voice hardened. "And if I run across them, I'll make sure they do just that."

"What's a jimmy?" she asked distractedly as they walked toward the porch.

"A short crowbar. It takes no finesse at all. No brains, either. Just muscles."

Kerry shivered again. "So what do we do now? Call the police?"

"Why bother? Our visitors didn't get in, and nothing was taken. The police can't do anything tonight that I can't do tomorrow. I'll have one of my men drop by to see about prints." He held the screen door open for her. "But just to keep things legal, I'll file a report tomorrow while I'm in town."

"What if they come back tonight?"

Devin studied her worried frown. "Changed your mind about the animals?"

"It's amazing what a crunched window does for one's perspective," she said dryly. "And don't gloat. It's not nice. So what if they do?"

"Come back? I wish they'd try."

"I'm serious."

"So am I."

"Devin—"

"Don't worry. You'll be safe. They'd have to go through me to get to you."

Kerry blinked. She supposed his grim voice was meant to be reassuring. It wasn't. "Thank you," she said politely, "but it wasn't my skin I was worried about. I was thinking about the house. I don't want anything else damaged."

Devin gave an indifferent shrug. "Same thing applies. They'd still have to get through me. As clumsy as they are, I'd hear them before they got very far." He studied her face, frowning at the strained look in her eyes. "Why don't you go on to bed. I'll finish checking the second floor before I turn in."

Devin lay with his hands tucked behind his head, gazing at the shifting pattern of moonlight on the wall while he thought of Kerry. He didn't need to see or hear her to know that she was prowling restlessly around her room, trying to cope with the adrenaline flooding her body. He knew exactly what was happening.

He could feel it.

He had a lot of experience in that area. He had spent a lifetime being linked to Megan, sharing her emotions, knowing when she was in trouble, being a part of her.

She was his twin, his other half. Was she still? he wondered. Or was he linked to both of them now? Because there was no doubt he was connected with Kerry. The pain shooting up his foot when the hammer had dropped on hers was a pretty clear indication, he thought wryly. That and his sleepless night, as well as a day spent being a receptor for her swinging emotions. He had no idea what had caused the emotions, but he'd known they were there. It had played hell with his concentration.

He grinned in the darkness of the room, wondering how Kerry felt about psychic linking.

It was more to the point in this situation to wonder how *he* felt about it, he realized after a moment. The bond with Megan had begun at birth, it had always been a part of him, a part he had accepted without question. Now he was apparently starting all over again with a new woman. A woman who sizzled with energy, who didn't seem to know the meaning of serenity. A small woman with the heart of a lion, a woman who would undoubtedly turn his life upside down.

Devin's smile faded. He wanted Kerry. One look was all it had taken to know that. But he wanted her as a woman, not necessarily a psychic mate. Maybe this whole thing was a mistake, he thought tiredly. A temporary aberration. A flutter or hiccup in the psychic wiring of the Murphy clan.

Devin awoke the next morning, inhaled the fragrance of freshly brewed coffee and decided there were worse ways to begin the day. Of course, if Kerry had wandered down during the night and crawled into bed beside him, things would have been even better.

Twenty minutes later, freshly showered and shaved, he walked into the large kitchen and found Kerry frowning over a small notebook. She was wearing a large, yellow T-shirt and snug, faded jeans. She apparently had decided the outfit was the kind that wouldn't attract male attention, he thought as she looked up with an absent smile. A platonic smile.

She was wrong. She could wear burlap sacks and men would still walk into walls while trying to get a better look at her.

Megan blinked as Devin poured himself a bowl of dry cereal, collected milk, a bagel, and a mug of coffee before sitting down beside her. Very close beside her.

She was going to have to do something about him, she reflected morosely. Fast. She hadn't had five hours of sleep in the past thirty-six and a good part of it was his fault. The gleam in his blue eyes was enough to set any woman on edge, because it said loud and clear that he had a lot more on his mind than security.

It wasn't going to be easy, she decided gloomily. For some reason, Megan—his sister, her boss—doted on the man. The only problem was that Megan saw him with a sister's eyes, not as a threat to a woman's peace of mind and a good night's sleep.

He was clad in gray slacks and a light blue shirt. A navy blazer hung over the doorknob. There wasn't a trench coat in sight. It wasn't her idea of detective garb, but what did she know? Maybe he was going to be tracking corporate executives all day.

"What's all that?" Devin nodded at several pages of notes she had spread before her.

"Things to do." She looked up with a frazzled air. "I have less than two months until the scheduled opening, and it's going to be close. I'm starting from scratch and the whole house, as well as the five cottages, have to be furnished from the floor up. Decisions have to be made about the windows, colors selected, and the kitchen completely outfitted."

"All that stuff Megan and Luke have in the warehouse should make it easier."

"It will, eventually. But first we have to go through a winnowing process. They bought period pieces that are appropriate for a one-hundred-year-old house, but since the other two plantations are as old as this one, not all the furniture will come here. First, I have to sort through it all with Megan and see how she wants it distributed, then I have to do some serious shopping."

"She's leaving it all up to you?"

Kerry nodded distractedly, scribbling another note to herself. "Megan is busy working on the second house. We'll have summit meetings, make decisions, but the job is mine."

"And are you, uh..." Devin ground to a stop and swore silently, wondering how to extricate his size eleven shoe from his mouth.

Kerry tilted her head and gave him a level glance. "What? Capable? Experienced?" She nodded briskly. "Yes. To all of your unasked—but still insulting—questions and doubts. It's in my genes, I suppose. I come from a long line of innkeepers, starting with my great-grandparents. Rooming houses, hotels, motels, inns, bed and breakfasts—you name it, I've done it.

I've also got degrees in business and hotel management."

She grinned when his eyes widened. "I told you not to be deceived by my baby face. Any other questions?"

Devin crunched thoughtfully on his granola and swallowed. "Yeah. What about men?"

"Men?" She touched the tip of her tongue to her upper lip. "What about them?"

"Man," he amended, delighted at the sign of nerves. "Singular. Will one be tagging along, determined to take you back to the mainland?"

Kerry shook her head. "Nope." She frowned as a thought occurred to her. "That is, not unless Jared and his wacko psychic find out where I am."

Devin stiffened. "What do you mean?"

"Have you ever heard of soulmates?" Kerry asked with a sigh.

"Sure. Who hasn't?"

"*I* hadn't until Jared entered my life—complete with his psychic, of course."

"Sounds fascinating," he said blandly, blue eyes appraising her exasperated expression as he took another mouthful of cereal.

"Weird," she corrected. "Extremely bizarre. And a long, dull story."

"I take it you're not exactly fascinated with the paranormal?"

"You take it right. I wouldn't touch that stuff with the proverbial ten-foot pole. I like to keep my feet firmly on the ground, thank you."

He acknowledged her brisk tone with a nod and bit a chunk out of the bagel. That pretty well answered his question about how she'd react to being psychically linked with him, he reflected wryly. She'd blow higher than Mauna Loa.

"I'm meeting with a couple of new clients today," he said, standing and dropping a business card on the table. "This is my office number. If you need me for anything, they can get through to me. And I'll have someone come out to dust the windows for prints."

Kerry nodded, watching him shrug into his jacket. "Tell them to help themselves. I probably won't be here. I'm going to be doing a dry run on the stores in town."

"Okay." He opened the screen door and stepped out onto the back porch, turning back to gaze at her. "I might have someone out here to do some measurements for the alarm system. I'll give him a key."

"Don't bother. I'm leaving the doors and windows open just in case those jerks come back. That way, they can get in the house without breaking anything."

"Kerry?"

"Hmm?" She kept her gaze on the blank page before her so she wouldn't get snared in those blue eyes.

"Take care of yourself."

She sighed. "I always do."

"And, Kerry..."

"What?"

"Don't slug anybody with a hammer."

She bared her teeth at him. "Funny. Very funny." She took refuge in the blank page again.

"Kerry?"

Her head snapped up. The man was going to drive her crazy. "What...do...you...want?"

"You," he said evenly. "Until it hurts."

Kerry watched in stunned amazement as the screen closed behind him. She didn't move until his Blazer started and growled its way down the road.

There was no doubt about it, she decided with a blink. Crazy. Definitely.

Three

"Hello?" Kerry grimaced at the telephone, aware that her breathless response wasn't exactly the poised, professional greeting one would expect from the manager of a business. It sounded more like the rattled voice of a woman whose house has just been broken into. For a second time.

Or perhaps broken into wasn't the precise term, she reflected, trying to catch her breath after the sprint downstairs from her tumbled bedroom. A pragmatic policeman or private investigator might say that a house whose resident had driven away leaving the doors and windows unlocked had been an open invitation to any lurking criminals. She had little doubt that was exactly what they would say, and since she wasn't in the mood for a lecture, she was seriously considering not telling them. Him.

"Kerry? What's the matter?" Devin's brusque voice broke through her mental monologue.

Speak of the devil, she thought with a grimace. "Devin? Oh...hi," she said brightly. "Are you catching your quota of bad guys today?"

"I think you've got me mixed up with the cops. Are you okay?"

"Okay?" she repeated cautiously. "Why wouldn't I be?"

"Kerry, I'm in the middle of something here and I'm not in the mood to play guessing games. Has anything happened at the house?"

What was going on? she wondered, searching for a safe, non-incriminating response. Did the blasted man have a crystal ball? Besides, now that she'd had time to catch her breath, she was almost convinced that the mess upstairs was the work of kids. It had nothing to do with the hotel break-in on another island. Kids were curious and would consider any empty house a challenge, Kerry assured herself.

With the sun beaming down and a balmy breeze jiggling the palm fronds, it was hard to accept Devin's more sinister assumption of local thugs. Even the damaged windows weren't necessarily the proof he considered them to be, she decided optimistically. Kids could have gotten at them with screwdrivers. Or something.

"I'm fine," she finally said. "I've only been back a few minutes." Just long enough to take her packages upstairs and find her dresser drawers pulled out, the contents dumped on her bed. And to be scared out of her wits for a few seconds. Just thinking about it made her pulse pound.

"Kerry?"

She sighed. He didn't believe her, and she supposed she couldn't blame him. They had both agreed that she was a rotten liar. What was worse, he had persistence honed to a fine art. Intimidation, too. She stared thoughtfully at the floor, wondering how long she could stall him and if it was worth the effort. Probably not. She had a nasty suspicion that he'd get the truth out of her one way or another.

Kerry's gaze sharpened and she stepped away from the counter to peer down at marks she hadn't noticed in her rush to answer the phone—a dusty trail of large shoe prints across the tiled floor. Her heart lurched and she decided that optimist or not, it was hard to cling to her bored-kids theory while gazing at the crisscross tread of a grown man's running shoe.

"Kerry, for God's sake, what's—"

"Devin," she whispered shakily into the mouthpiece, "you're right. Something *has* happened and I'm getting out of here. Meet you at your office." Without giving him a chance to respond, she hung up the phone, grabbed her bag from the counter, threw a quick glance over her shoulder and dashed for the door.

Devin stared blankly at the telephone and swore. She'd hung up on him. In a rage, he slammed the instrument down, stalked to the door and threw it open. She had hung up on him.

His secretary, a small woman with dark hair and a cheerful smile, glanced up from the newspaper she was reading and pursed her lips in a silent whistle. "Let me guess. Your hard drive crashed again."

Devin glared at her. Everyone in the office knew he had a love-hate relationship with his computer. Joanie was the only one who teased him about it. She was, of course, a cousin.

"I have good news for you," she told him brightly, waving at the daily paper. "If you want to do some ambulance-chasing, you have your choice of two murders, a robbery, and a series of dognappings around the islands. Probably make some big bucks."

"I've got more work than I can handle now and you know it. If you're going to read the paper on the job, at least don't make any crack-brained excuses for doing it. Kerry Cottrell is on her way over," he said grimly. "I want to see her the second she gets here."

"Yes, *sir*. Who is she?"

"The new manager of Rainbow's End."

"What's she like?" Joanie asked with blatant curiosity. "Is she the one who lit your fuse?"

"Don't keep her out here talking," he told her, ignoring her questions. When he'd hired Joanie, he had threatened her with dismemberment if she ever discussed their cases outside the office. She had said she understood, and he'd believed her. But since she considered all personal matters grist for the family mill, he made it a point to keep his private life private. "And tell Brandon I want to see him before he leaves for Rainbow's End."

"Will do. By the way, while you were out you got a call from a Mrs. Conroy. A very upset lady. I told her you'd call this afternoon."

"About what?"

"She wants you to find Fred." She grinned. "Her dog."

"Joanie, for God's sake! Call her back and tell her I'm busy."

"Uh, Dev?"

"What?"

She grimaced. "I kind of told her you'd do it."

"You *what?*"

"I'm sorry. I know I shouldn't have, but she was crying. Fred's the only thing she has—besides a lot of money. I'll never do it again, I promise." She waited nervously, then added, "Please?"

Devin looked at her pleading expression and swore, long and colorfully. "I'll call her, but damn it, Joanie—"

She held up her hand in a peaceful gesture. "I know...never again."

He glared at her and went back to his office.

He was still grimly furious twenty minutes later when Kerry tapped on the door. He flung it open, hooked a large hand around her arm and hauled her in the office. Closing the door behind them, he tugged her closer and wrapped his arms around her, burying her face in his chest and holding her so tight she gasped.

"Don't you ever, *ever,* hang up on me again," he muttered in her hair.

"Mmmpf." Kerry planted her fists on his chest and pushed. When she managed to pull back a couple of inches, she noted with satisfaction that her lipstick had stained his shirt. It served him right, she decided with a scowl. "What on earth is the matter with you?" she demanded, stepping on his toe for good measure.

"You are."

She gave him a swift, assessing glance and didn't like what she saw. If he had simply been worried, she could have handled it, but he'd passed that stage and was hovering somewhere between protective and outright possessive. Pushing him again, she panted, "You act like a Neanderthal and it's *my* fault? I think not. Let me go."

When he dropped his arms, Kerry prudently backed away before planting her fists on her hips. "I don't know what's going on here—" she flung out her hand in a gesture that included the two of them "—but I don't like it any more than I like people pawing through my things."

"I know, honey," Devin soothed, eyeing her cautiously, surprised by the temper blazing in her eyes. He put his own anger on the back burner, deciding he'd get back to it when she calmed down. "It takes a while to get over these things. You're still dealing with the shock of the hotel break-in."

"The heck I am." Kerry perched on the corner of his desk, frowning at him. His pacifying tone annoyed her as much as his anger had. "And don't call me honey. I'm mad, not shocked. And I'm entitled. It's been less than an hour since someone pulled all my clothes out of the dresser and closet. I'm getting tired of finding my room trashed."

She took a quick, assessing look around the large room while he swore. Oak cabinets, glass-topped desk and a computer setup that could launch the starship *Enterprise*. The high-rent district had taken her by surprise, but should have prepared her for an office suitable for any high-powered businessman. It was a far cry from the cramped room she'd imagined, with a trench coat thrown over a chair back and a bottle of Scotch in a desk drawer.

"Damn it." Devin stepped closer, looking ready to strangle her. "There *was* something wrong when I called. I knew it. I—"

"How did you know?"

The quiet question stopped him. Her tone didn't invite an honest reply any more than her cool expression did, he decided, assessing the suspicion in her hazel eyes. This was the lady who lumped psychics right along with frauds and weirdos, he reminded himself. A woman running from a ''bizarre'' boyfriend. Devin gave her a small smile and did the only thing he could think of. He stalled.

''What?''

''How did you know something was wrong?'' she repeated.

Devin shrugged and looked right into her watchful eyes. ''Your voice. It was a dead giveaway.''

''Oh.''

''Private investigators catch things like that if they're any good. And I'm good, honey. Very good.''

His husky voice sent a shiver down her spine. She had no doubt that he was. Good. Very good. At any number of things. Things that weren't necessarily part of catching bad guys. Things that a woman who hadn't gotten a handle on the male-female stuff by the time she'd turned twenty-seven might just find out of her league.

''You didn't hear my voice until I answered,'' she noted in a reasonable voice.

''True.''

''So why did you call?''

''Call?''

''Call.'' Her brows rose in exasperation. ''Me. On the phone. Just when my blood was roaring through my veins because I thought some creep had broken into my room again.''

''And had one?''

Kerry winced. His voice was soft. Too soft. "It's possible," she admitted reluctantly.

"How possible?"

"Very." She told him about the footprints in the kitchen. "I knew they weren't yours because you had on leather-soled shoes this morning."

"And how did he get in?"

"I left the place open." She gave him a tentative smile.

"You..." He stopped. Tilting his head to one side, he eyed her as if she were an alien form that had landed on the island during the night. He tried again. "You left it open?"

Kerry nodded. "I told you this morning that I was going to." She shifted, crossing her ankles, waiting for the other shoe to fall. It didn't take long.

"I thought you were kidding. You left the house *open?*"

She nodded again, watching the temper in his blue eyes.

"I bust my butt keeping that place secure, and the first day you're on the job you leave it unlocked? Tell me something, are you going to make that a habit?"

"You're upset." She sighed.

"Upset? Brilliant. But wrong. What I am is mad, damned mad. What the hell do you mean by—"

Kerry held up a hand to stop him. "All right. Be mad. Stay mad. But just listen to me. There's nothing in the house worth taking, right?"

He gave a tight nod.

"It just made sense to let this idiot come in and find out for himself. I don't see any point in allowing him to ruin doors and windows—"

"Made *sense?*" he interrupted ruthlessly, moving until he towered over her. He shoved his hands into his pockets to keep from wrapping them around her neck and got some small satisfaction when her eyes widened in alarm. Not a lot, but some.

She gave him a wary look but stuck to her guns. "Yes, sense. Now that he's gotten in and found an empty house, there's no reason for him to come back."

"I can think of one." He moved back, giving them both room, because if he stayed close enough to breathe in the fragrance of her—the fresh, clear scent of wildflowers—he would strangle her. Or kiss her. And he had a gut feeling that she'd object as strenuously to one act as the other.

Kerry frowned. "What reason?"

"You."

"Me?"

Her look of disbelief maddened him. "We've been assuming that he's a thief. We could be wrong. Dead wrong. He could have been standing behind your bedroom door, waiting for you."

Kerry shivered at the grim little scenario, then her common sense kicked in. "Devin, I'm not the type of woman who drives men mad with lust." She looked up in time to catch the speculation on his face and narrowed her eyes in warning. "Now you're asking me to believe that someone saw me on Oahu, broke into my room, found me gone and tossed my clothes around to express his disappointment? And to further believe that the exact same thing is happening here on the Big Island?" She shook her head. "No way. Not to me."

Devin gazed at her, baffled. She believed it. He saw the certainty in her expression and knew she believed every word. Wondering how she'd explain the ache that gnawed at him every time he thought of her, the hunger that had slammed at him the first time he'd seen her, he held out his hand to her and waited. When her fingers touched his, his grip tightened, tugged, and he waited for her to slip off the desk. He led her to the chair beside his desk and waited again. When she sat, so did he.

"I can think of another possibility," he told her.

Kerry groaned. "I just bet you can. You probably have a hundred of them, each one grimmer than the last. Okay, I'll bite. What?"

"He's a rapist." Which wasn't all that different from the first, he thought. She had just jumped to the wrong conclusion.

Kerry gazed at him, fascinated. "You have a twisted mind, Murphy. Your work is really getting to you. I like my idea better. I think it's kids."

"Wearing big shoes?"

"Oh, I forgot about that."

"You want to forget about it."

Her fascination turned to resentment. "Sure I do. Wouldn't you?" She sighed. "Okay, what's the story on this one? Since rape is a crime of violence rather than sex, I take off my temptress hat and become an innocent tourist, in the wrong place at the wrong time?" She frowned at him. "I don't think so. We still have two islands, two break-ins and . . . what? A man who hopped a plane to follow me here?"

His blood ran cold at the thought. Kerry wasn't taking the situation or him seriously, but he had seen too many cases of violence in a head-on collision with the innocent, the unsuspecting. He didn't care how much noise she made, how much of a fight she put up, he wasn't going to let it happen here. Not to her.

Kerry shook her head. "I don't buy it. I don't buy any of it. I think this is a real case of a molehill and a mountain. Besides—" She stopped and gave him an expectant glance.

"Besides what?"

She checked her watch. "I think it's time for lunch."

Lunch, he thought in disbelief. Then he caught a flicker of hope in her eyes and knew she didn't want food nearly as much as she wanted to change the subject. "Okay, who's buying?"

"You are." She gave him a victorious smile. "The way I figure it, I got you a bed, so you owe me."

"Okay." He got to his feet. "Lunch is on me, but don't look so smug. We're going to have a long discussion about burglary statistics—with locked and unlocked doors."

Kerry looked up at him as he headed for the door. "You're a hard man, Murphy."

"You've got that right, babe," he muttered.

"My name isn't babe." She took another quick look around. "You don't happen to have a bottle of Scotch in the office, do you?"

"I hate the stuff."

"Another illusion shattered."

"Since you're so chatty, let's move. I know a nice quiet place where we can talk."

Kerry groaned.

"When it comes to business, there's nothing like a little good, old-fashioned nepotism."

Kerry gave a satisfied sigh and looked across the width of the rented sofa at Devin, tapping her fingernail on the neatly typed list of names he had given her. Outside, the full moon threw enough light to read by. Inside the spacious room, several lamps did the same job.

"Are you sure these are all of the relatives you have in business around here? This is great to start with, but they're all in retail or rentals. What about services?"

She held up a hand, counting on her fingers. "I'll need a laundry—one that picks up and delivers—an exterminator, and window cleaners right away. Also, a cook and a couple of maids."

Devin groaned. "Joanie spent most of the afternoon pulling these out of Megan's Rolodex. Now you want me to tell her to start all over again?"

Megan's grin held no sympathy. "Unless you want me to ignore the family." Her smile faded as she eyed him thoughtfully. "The McCalls have given me a free hand on this, but I need to tell you the same thing I told them. This is a business, and I don't deal with incompetents. Family members will be given a chance, but I get comparative bids and I expect quality service."

"Anything else?" Devin turned his head and gazed at the darkness beyond the window, waiting for her reply. He had been right about her. She seemed to run in only one gear—high. This was just her second day in the house and she was already up to her eyebrows in lists. She was also jittery because things weren't moving faster. Her impatience and frustration nudged at him, made him almost as edgy as she was.

"Anything else? You bet." She grinned at his resigned expression. "Are any of the cousins car dealers? I want to turn in my rental and get something snazzy."

"Why bother?" Devin reached for the pitcher of iced tea and refilled their glasses, stirred by her smile and tamping down the feeling. "Luke said he'd get a car out here in a couple of days."

"I know. A business car, probably a van. We'll use it for shopping and picking up an occasional guest, but I want my own." Her eyes sparkled. "Red, low and fast."

Devin winced. "You wouldn't settled for something with a lower profile, I suppose. Like a tan sedan?"

"Give me a break, Murphy. Even my grandmother doesn't drive a car like that. Nope." Her smile was full of anticipation. "Hot and fast, that's the way I like them." Her grin faded when she took a closer look at his grim profile. "I suppose you have a reason for asking," she said, knowing he was going to spoil her good mood.

"If someone is following you, I'd just like to make it a little harder."

Kerry shook her head. "I'm not convinced that anyone is. But even if you're right, he already knows where he can find me, so I don't see that it makes any difference what I'm driving."

"Maybe you're right."

"No maybe about it."

"Kerry?"

"Hmm?" She lifted her gaze from the list of his relatives.

"I want to talk to you."

Kerry groaned. "Again? Whatever happened to strong, silent men? All you've done when we're together is talk. Lecture, actually. What now? What can you possibly have missed?"

"This," Devin murmured. He leaned forward, crowding her, pleased when he saw sudden understanding widen her hazel eyes. Excitement. Alarm. Confusion. They jolted her, made her retreat. He followed.

"Talk," she said hurriedly, putting a hand on his chest to stop him. "Great idea. You first."

"I changed my mind." He tugged the papers from her hand and let them slip to the floor. "I said it all this morning."

You. Until it hurts.

The words had haunted her all day, danced in her mind, jiggled her nerves. Through errands, telephone calls, and a possible attempted burglary, they had delighted and terrified her.

A woman would have to be dead not to respond to the message behind the words. A man of extraordinary strength and determination—not to mention smoldering sexuality—had looked at her and liked what he'd seen. Wanted what he'd seen. Was there a woman alive who could resist the focused concentration of those blue eyes?

She doubted it.

On the other hand, the same man had a take-charge, me-Tarzan, you-little-woman mentality that would send a modern-day feminist screaming into the night. A woman would be crazy to let him take over her life. Because that was exactly what he would do. He would make the decisions, give the orders and raise the roof if they weren't followed to the letter. All because he was male, taller and broader.

On the other hand...

Devin looked down at her, wondering what was going on behind those gorgeous eyes. Whatever it was, it was driving him crazy. Her pupils enlarged, leaving a narrow rim of gold-shot green and turquoise. Her soft breath warmed his cheek.

"Kerry?"

"What?" Her reply was soft, practically a whisper.

"About this morning."

Her heart gave a bounce of alarm. She didn't want to have a meaningful conversation about that. She didn't want an explanation. Or an example. What Kerry wanted more than anything was to forget the whole thing. She prodded his chest with a slim finger and tried to move him back a few inches. When he stayed right where he was, she said brightly, "Don't give it another thought. At one time or another we all say things we don't mean. It's okay, I understand."

"I don't think you do."

Shaking her head, Kerry said, "You're wrong. I do. I really do. Sometimes words—the wrong ones—just have a way of... popping out."

"Not out of me they don't." Devin grinned. Alarm. Retreat. Resistance. They zinged around her, cutting her air supply, coloring her cheeks. She was flustered, determined not to show it—and absolutely adorable. He eased back a bit to see what she'd do.

Kerry moved. Quick as a cat, she jumped to her feet and crossed to the window. Tact, she decided. That's what she needed. To be tactful and firm. Get it over with. Settle it now before it turned into another mess. She thought fleetingly of Charles and Jared and knew she was right.

"I meant it," Devin said in a level voice. "Every word."

"Too bad." To hell with tact, she decided abruptly, seeing the determined gleam in his eyes. In this case it was useless. This had nothing to do with him being the boss's brother. This was man-and-woman stuff. Probably too much man and not enough woman. Whatever. She was going to put a stop to it. Here and now. Pleased that her tone matched his, she added for good measure, "I'm not interested."

"You will be."

The arrogant knothead. Anger shot through Kerry, making her head pound. She took a steadying breath and leaned back, tightening her hands on the sill. "I doubt it." She shook her head slowly. "I'm here to do a job. A good one. That's all I'm interested in."

Devin leaned back and gave her a bland smile. "You won't be working all the time."

"Enough to keep me busy. Too busy to be distracted."

"And I'd be a distraction?"

You betcha. "Not just you," she said coolly. "Anyone would be." He didn't like that, she noted with satisfaction, watching his eyes narrow. Not one little bit. While she had the advantage, she asked bluntly, "Why me?"

Good question, Devin thought, taking in her frazzled expression. A damn good one. Why not one of the many attractive women he'd dated over the years? Why not someone he'd known all his life? It was a question that deserved an answer, he reflected, wondering if she'd settle for *because*.

He shrugged. "Why not?"

"Why *not*?" Kerry pushed away from the window and stomped over to him, throwing up her hands in exasperation. "I'll tell you why not. Because you don't know a thing about me, that's why not." She glared down at him. "How long have you lived on this island?"

"All of my life, give or take a few years." His gaze met hers and he could feel the energy sizzling through her.

"And how many people do you know here?"

"A lot."

"How many women do you know?"

The corners of his mouth turned up. He knew exactly where she was heading. He also knew it wouldn't do a damn bit of good. "A lot."

"How well do you know them? Most of them," she amended.

"Very well."

"Ah! Well, there you have it."

"What do I have?"

Her frown turned into an outright scowl. Speaking slowly, as if to a simpleton, she said, "You have knowledge, something in common, that's what you have. Go call one of them."

Devin shook his head. "Won't work."

"*What* won't work, for heaven's sake?"

"It's not the same." He wanted to laugh at her look of utter exasperation. She had a temper, usually kept on a short rein, but it was there. He shot a quick glance around the room, empty of the usual accessories and knickknacks. If there had been anything close at hand, he knew with certainty that she'd be heaving it at him.

"I don't believe this," Kerry muttered, pacing up and down in front of him. Stopping, she jammed her fists on her hips and glared at him. "What's different about me? Just name one thing."

Devin gazed at her, taking in her simmering challenge. *You're summer lightning, wildfire, enchantment, rainbows. Volcanoes. The scent of wildflowers. Miracles. And you're mine.*

Getting to his feet, he smiled. "Let's just say you're... unique. I think I'll turn in now. I checked everything, so all you have to do is get the lights." He moved toward the door, wondering how far he'd get before she stopped him.

"Devin?"

"Um?"

"That wasn't an answer. It doesn't make sense."

"Then we'll discuss it again. Later." He looked over his shoulder. "Did I tell you our bosses are concerned about your visitor today?"

She blinked. "Megan? And Luke?"

"Yeah. They don't want you out here alone, so I'm moving my computer in tomorrow and setting up a temporary office."

"You're *what?*"

"Just until you get some guests on a regular basis."

"But—"

"It won't be too bad. I do a lot of my business on the telephone and computer, so it'll work. When I have to be away, we'll make other arrangements."

"But—"

"My room is big enough for a desk and the files I'll need."

"But—"

"Don't worry. I'll keep the confusion to a minimum. You can just work around me."

"But—"

"See you in the morning." He gave her one last nod and headed down the hall for his room. Grinning, he closed the door on her outraged shriek.

"Damn it, Devin, come back here. We're talking about *two months*."

Four

A week later Devin sat in front of his computer in his makeshift office, running his fingers swiftly over the keyboard while he balanced the phone with a hunched shoulder. The flood of morning sunlight was held at bay by a stretch of vertical blinds.

"Okay, Joanie, tell Brandon I want him to check on social security numbers for everyone on the list."

"Will do. Uh, Dev? Before you go, Mrs. Conroy called. You know, the one—"

"With Fred, the gray poodle. Tell her we're still looking."

"That's the thing. We don't have to."

"He came back?"

"Well . . . sort of. Today."

"Good."

"I guess. You're not going to be real thrilled with this, but she got a ransom note."

Devin's fingers stilled on the keyboard as he focused his attention on Joanie's voice. "She paid it?"

"Five thousand bucks' worth."

"Why the hell didn't she call me?"

"She did. Just now."

His hand tightened on the receiver. "I mean before she paid."

"Because she wanted Fred back," Joanie said reasonably. "I hate to tell you this, Dev, but not everybody's concerned about catching crooks. At least, not until they take care of number one."

"I'll call her," he said grimly. "No one shakes down one of my clients. "Give me her number and—" Devin stopped, wincing as a whip of fury came out of nowhere. The intensity left him breathless. "I've got to go," he said tightly.

"Devin, are you okay?"

"I'll call you back." He dropped the phone and headed for the back door. "Kerry?" He swore steadily as he moved through the still empty rooms. Damn it, she was going to drive him crazy before another day was over, he decided, throwing open the screen and leaping down the stairs.

He vaulted over a wheelbarrow left by the gardener, barely clearing the hoe and shovel next to it. She had turned his life upside down. Instead of an orderly office, he was working on a wing and a prayer in a temporary bedroom. Instead of peace and quiet, he was invaded by her energy and buffeted by her emotions.

Sleep was a lost luxury. Just last night he had been jolted awake by a flash of terror. He'd run down stairs, enough adrenaline pumping through him to take down a platoon of junkies. Instead, he'd found her in the living room, watching in horror as a gecko skittered over the wall. She'd stared at the miniature lizard as if it were a prehistoric monster and demanded that Devin take it outside.

Yeah, there was no doubt about it, the last week had been chaos. He grinned. And he wouldn't have missed a second of it.

"Kerry?" Even so, it wasn't getting any better... or easier. Several times a day her raw, unfiltered feelings jumped headfirst into his psyche and, regardless of the emotion, the force of it hit him with the impact of a sledgehammer to the gut.

"*Kerry?* Damn it, answer me!" He veered to the left, not questioning the fact he was heading for the newly constructed garage that held his truck, his gray BMW and her new car. On some instinctive level, he always knew where she was. He slowed down to a trot before he turned the corner of the garage, certain now that she was safe.

Thanks to his years of practice with Megan, he had a fair handle on the situation, he thought grimly. Once he set aside his initial reaction to the blast of emotion, he simply let the feelings wash over him. He never knew what initiated them, but he was good at reading them. Unfortunately, the negative ones were always the strongest.

He caught up with her in the garage and found exactly what he'd expected to find. She was mad. Actually, she was steaming—but she wasn't in any danger.

"Kerry?" His blue gaze went over her in one hard, comprehensive sweep that took in her white shirt with rolled-up sleeves, yellow shorts and flimsy sandals. No signs of damage, he noted automatically. No mussed hair, no torn clothes, no blood.

What there was plenty of was sheer, riotous indignation. No, scratch that, he decided after another quick glance. Fury. Hot, impotent fury.

"Just how ham-handed are those guys from the security company?" she demanded, turning to glare at him.

"Only as much as they need to be, I suppose." His voice was level, an instinctive reaction, even though he felt the back of his neck prickle. The company was the best on the island, and he knew their track record. They were clean and competent. "Why?"

"Because someone's been messing with my car."

The tension in his shoulders eased. "Honey," he drawled, "that's what you get when you buy low, hot and fast." Snazzy was what she'd wanted and snazzy was what she got—a candy-red Corvette. "A car like that will always draw men, even without you in it."

With her fists planted on her hips and her eyes shooting golden fire, she looked like a young Amazon, he thought, moving closer. "You can't blame a guy for looking, and dreaming a little."

Kerry's eyes narrowed. "They can look all they want. They can dream all they want. They can even touch and get fingerprints all over it, but I draw the line at breaking windows."

"What?" He wrapped his fingers around her arm and tugged her closer, keeping her next to him as he circled the car. "They didn't do this." His voice was hard.

"How do you know?"

He shrugged. "They didn't have to. If they'd needed anything in the car—which they didn't—they would have asked for the key." He slid his hand down her arm, lacing his fingers with hers. "Besides, this was done by amateurs."

She stiffened. "And they're pros, I suppose."

"Damned straight. I wouldn't have hired them if they weren't." He stopped at the driver's door, studying the cracked window. "This is the only one damaged. Looks like something spooked him and he took off. Damn it, Kerry, I don't like it. Not one bit."

"Not nearly as much as I don't," she assured him. "If I could get my hands on whoever did it, I'd—"

"You'd leave him to me," he told her flatly.

Kerry gave him a quick sideways glance. "I would?"

"You would," he assured her. "If you value that gorgeous hide of yours, you would. Come on." He turned toward the house. "I'll make another police report and then we'll talk."

Thirty minutes later he found Kerry sitting cross-legged on the living room floor, surrounded by boxes of linens. She was ripping off the plastic wrap and stacking sheets by color.

She looked like a princess caught in a rainbow. Without warning, hunger gripped him, almost knocking him flat. He wanted her, and he knew damn well he would have her. And, he promised himself, it wouldn't be much longer.

"Kerry?"

"Umm?" She looked up, her eyes widening as she watched his expression change from wonder to a deep, electrifying awareness ... from awareness to hunger ... from hunger to sheer possession. And determination. Lord, yes, she thought with a shiver, the determination. As his gaze skimmed over her, then met hers, she felt every muscle in her body melting.

"Blue sheets are king size, yellow—queen, and white—twin," she mumbled distractedly, wondering how a woman was expected to deal with a gaze like that.

Never in her life had anyone looked at her in just that way. Never had she been the object of such focused intensity. A blue gaze that held all the heat in the world moved on to her mouth, lingered and made promises that sent fire spiraling through her body.

"We've got to talk," Devin said abruptly.

"Talk?" She wasn't ready for a chat just then. Casual or any other kind. And if his words were going to reflect the sizzling look in his eyes, she might *never* be ready.

On the other hand, she reflected darkly, he had kept her on an emotional roller coaster for a solid week, and that was precisely one week too long. She had come to the island expecting hard work and long hours, but she hadn't expected a man like Devin to be part of the package. A man far more dangerous than either of the two she had recently walked away from.

But nothing was going to make her walk—or run—again. Not inept burglars and especially not a man with hunger in his eyes. So if a simple conversation would settle the matter, she decided, they would talk.

"Okay," she agreed, slapping a yellow sheet on the growing pile before she looked up at him. "Have a seat." She gestured at the floor. "I can't think when people loom over me like that."

When he settled down across from her, she gazed at him thoughtfully. He leaned back against the wall, crossed his arms across his chest and took a deep breath, ready to jump right in. "You have a habit of popping up whenever something happens around here," she said, beating him to the punch. "How much of it is an accident?"

His brows rose. "Are you asking me if I jimmied the dining room windows and tried to break into your car?"

She waved away the question, shaking her head. "No. If you'd done it, it would have been done right."

"Thanks," he said dryly. "I think."

"I'm not sure what I'm asking." Her eyes narrowed in thought. "It's simply that you have an uncanny knack of calling or arriving just when things get tense. How do you do it?"

Devin shrugged. "I don't know." And he didn't. He'd lived with it all of his life and he still didn't understand it, which was all to the good as far as he was concerned—at least for right now. At least as far as Kerry was concerned. The longer he kept her away from words like *intuition* and *psychic ability,* the better off they'd both be. "Gut instinct and sheer luck, I guess. It's part of my stock-in-trade as a hotshot detective."

She shot him a dubious look. "You mean while other detectives follow clues and do a lot of slogging around, you just listen to a little voice?"

"Not *just*," he corrected. "As well as. I do my share of clue-digging and slogging, too. Which brings us back to the point of this little chat. What do you have that someone wants?"

Kerry's eyes widened. "Me? You're saying all this stuff is my fault? Some idiot breaks into my car, and I'm to blame?"

"We're not talking about whose fault it is, we're trying to find out why it's being done."

"So why look at me?"

"Because there's nowhere else to look. Someone broke into your room in Oahu, but didn't take anything. That tells me he didn't find what he wanted. When you leave and come here—to a place that up to then had been completely ignored by break-in artists—someone hacks away at the windows, strolls through the house when you're gone and tries to get in your car. So you tell me where I should look."

"You have a nasty way of making a point," Kerry grumbled. "But I don't like it."

"Neither do I."

"It doesn't make sense." She gave him a belligerent look, ready for an argument.

"Puzzles rarely do, at first." He took a small notebook out of his pocket. "Okay, Kerry, talk to me."

She blinked. "About what?"

"Anything you think might have some bearing on what's happening."

"I—" Her parted lips closed, stopping her automatic denial. After several moments of thought, she shook her head. "Devin, I'm trying to help, but I honestly can't think of a thing. When I was at the hotel, I only had a suitcase with vacation clothes, a couple of books and my camera. No valuables of any kind. I brought the same stuff with me when I came here. That's what I'm using until my things arrive from San Francisco."

"Family?"

Kerry stiffened. "What about them? Surely you don't think they're involved."

"Come on, Kerry. Maybe there's someone out there who doesn't like them and decided to hassle you just for the hell of it. Give me something to work with."

She sighed sharply. "My parents are Dennis and Margaret Cottrell. They own a bed and breakfast in the wine country. Napa Valley. And I won't have you upsetting them, you hear?"

"I hear." His voice was soothing. "Anyone else?"

"My grandmother, Amy Cottrell. She has a motel in the same area."

"I won't upset her, either."

"Is that it?" she asked hopefully, then groaned when he waggled his notebook at her.

"Any enemies?"

She didn't have to give that one any more thought than the others. Shaking her head, she said, "Nope. Not a one."

Devin raised his brows and waited.

Kerry gave an exasperated sigh. "Look, I don't know what kind of people you're used to dealing with, but I don't go through life cutting others down and walking on them. I assume you're talking about something more serious than a grocer trying to pad a bill or a plumber overcharging."

"Yeah, I am."

She shook her head again. "Nothing. No one. Next?"

"Men."

Kerry bristled. And somehow managed to look defensive and militant at the same time. "Men? As in..."

"Lovers? Disgruntled?"

Kerry reached for another set of sheets and absently plucked at the plastic covering. "No lovers," she finally said.

That wasn't what the check he'd run on her had disclosed. There was a college affair and a broken engagement that he knew of. "Ever?" Devin asked blandly.

"Lately," she amended. "In the last year or so. Oh, I've dated a couple of men, but neither are the type to—"

"How did you end things? Amicably?" When she hesitated, he frowned. "Names?"

"For heaven's sake, Devin! They're just ordinary men, not serial murderers."

"Fine. Give me the names, and I'll make sure they're not wandering around the island peeking in windows." He waited. "Kerry?"

Groaning at his implacable tone, she said, "Charles Atwood. He's a CPA and a pillar of the community. And I'll never forgive you if you embarrass me."

"Why? You planning to go back and pick up the pieces?"

She shook her head. "No way. It's over and done with, but he's a decent man. He doesn't deserve to be hassled just because we had a difference of opinion."

Devin looked up from the notepad. "What was the problem?" He almost grinned at her harassed expression.

"I don't know. Well, yes, I do. He wanted more from the relationship than I did. I thought I'd made it clear when we began dating that I wasn't looking for anything serious or permanent, but I guess I hadn't."

"Sounds like a sore loser to me."

"I thought so, too, until I had the exact same problem with Jared. Jared Mitchell," she added when he waggled his notebook at her again. "A shop owner and a model citizen. But I suppose I should have suspected something when I found out it was a meta-physical bookstore," she said darkly.

"And he wanted—"

"More than I did. He also came with a psychic sidekick who had convinced him that we were soul-mates."

"So you ended things?"

Kerry shrugged. "I tried to."

"But?"

"Suddenly he didn't understand the meaning of no. And he kept bringing me books about out-of-body experiences and finding soulmates. I was getting a lit-tle claustrophobic."

"So you decided to leave?"

"Not entirely because of Jared. The B and B I was managing was a small one. When I took the job, I told the owners that I would be wanting something bigger in a couple of years, and when Megan came with her offer, everything just fell in place."

"So you hightailed it out of Dodge because your... friend was too persistent?"

Her eyes flashed gold fire at him, but she said calmly enough, "I consider it a professional move."

"Okay," he said briskly, "who else is on the hit list?"

Kerry jumped to her feet and paced back and forth in front of him. "Damn it! There isn't a list—hit or any other kind. I don't believe for one second that ei-ther of those men would try to frighten or hurt me. And there's no one else." She stared down at him, fists on her hips. "No... one... else. Got that?"

"Fine." Devin reached up and snagged her wrist, wrapping his long fingers around it and tugging her down into his lap. "Then we'll try another approach. Tell me about your vacation."

Kerry gasped, torn between anger and astonishment—and a deep sense of facing the inevitable. "What are you doing?"

"Holding you."

"I know." Kerry shivered. All she could feel was Devin. His muscular thighs beneath her and his arm tightening around her waist. His heat. His touch. "Why?"

"Because I need to," he said simply.

She gave a tentative wiggle, trying to slide away. His arm kept her where she was. "Devin?"

"Hmm?"

"This isn't a smart thing to do."

"Could've fooled me. Why not?"

"Why *not?*" She tilted her head back to look at him and knew that she had made a mistake. A big one. His blue eyes were amused, inviting her to enjoy the moment, to enjoy him. But beyond the lazy gleam of laughter lay the real danger, she decided. The heat. The curiosity. And the promise.

She blinked, cutting off the connection. "Because," she said briskly, staring at his collar. "We're both here to do a job."

"Right. We'll call this a coffee break."

Kerry looked up again, an anxious frown etching a crease between her brows. "Devin, I don't know if I've been sending the wrong kind of messages—"

"I've read them just fine."

"I mean, I don't want you to think—"

"I don't."

"Then, why—"

"Because you're as curious as I am. You feel the tension as much as I do. Because I wanted to kiss you the first day I walked in here."

Kerry stared at him in disbelief. "The first day?"

"Actually, the first minute."

"That's crazy. No one takes one look and—"

"And I've waited eight days." His hand cupped the back of her neck, his fingers gentle, his grip steady. He watched the puzzled frown fade and alarm whip into her eyes. Fright would have stopped him dead, but along with the alarm, Kerry's eyes held an intensely feminine blend of curiosity and anticipation. An irresistible combination.

"Yeah, it's crazy all right. I should have done it then and got it out of my system." Devin lowered his head and when she stiffened, he stopped. "All you have to do is say no, Kerry. That's all you'll ever have to do."

"Damn you."

Her husky whisper was lost when his lips brushed hers. Brushed, came back and settled, taking her warmth, giving his. They curved in a small smile when her arms came up around his neck and hung on for dear life.

It was all there, he thought, his body jolting when her tongue met his in a small, erotic glide. The sweetness, the excitement, the slam of sex. He laced his fingers in her hair, removing pins, savoring the silky fall over his arm. All there. Wrapped in a body that had driven him crazy for a week. All there, from innocent joy to pure, instinctive seduction.

He was hard, she thought hazily as her body betrayed her by brazenly leaning into him. His arms, mouth, body, all hard and demanding. One callused hand worked up under her shirt, exploring, and she shivered when the crisp brownish red hair on his arms brushed her back.

Kerry nestled closer. It had been so long since she'd been held like this. So long since she'd cared whether she was held or not. When she parted her lips in invitation and he accepted, she acknowledged the truth. She had never been held like this.

She couldn't breathe. She didn't care. Couldn't think. Her schedule, her chores, her notes all faded away, disappeared, replaced by pure, thundering emotions. The feel of hard muscles beneath her fingers, the smell of him, a combination of soap and warm skin, the urgent murmur of his voice, the taste of his mouth, the race of their hearts.

And then, as suddenly as it began, it was over.

When Kerry looked up, there was stunned pleasure in her eyes. While she drew in a shaky breath, Devin touched her lower lip with his thumb. It was swollen and moist, and the heat built up in him until he thought he'd explode with need. He wanted to soothe it with his tongue, he wanted her, any way he could get her.

Kerry cleared her throat. "Like I said, that wasn't a good idea."

"I don't know. Seemed okay to me."

"Okay?"

He grinned at the flare of outrage in her eyes. "It settled one question. One kiss isn't enough to get you out of my system."

Kerry rolled off his lap and jumped to her feet. "That's too bad, because that was it."

"Just one to a customer?"

"It was one too many," she told him, busily dusting off the back of her shorts and avoiding his gaze. "I told you before, I'm here to work, not..."

"Have an affair?" he asked helpfully.

She wanted to hit him. Instead she met his teasing blue eyes full-on. "Exactly. Not to have an affair. Especially with the boss's brother."

He leaned back against the wall and gazed at her. "That bother you? Her being my sister?"

Kerry tapped her foot impatiently. "You're missing the point. What bothers me is being distracted when I have so much to do."

"So what you're saying is, you want to schedule our affair—when things are a little quieter." He grinned at her look of utter exasperation.

"What I want is to be left alone."

He might have believed her if he hadn't caught the edgy way she kept her distance. When a man had an active sixth sense and knew how to use it, and Devin did, he'd know that the edginess had nothing to do with dislike and everything to do with uneasiness. And the reason for that was found in her hazel eyes, in the remnants of passion that she couldn't quite conceal. In the shock waves that were still skittering through her body.

"Sorry," he said, finally breaking the tense silence. "I can't do that."

He didn't sound sorry. She frowned. "You can't do what?"

"Leave you alone. Be pretty hard to have that affair if I did."

Kerry's scowl deepened. "Look, just because I think you're... One kiss doesn't mean I'm jumping into bed with you."

"You can slide in," he told her, slowly getting to his feet. "You can do it any way you want as long as you do it. I won't even rush you. Take a couple of days to get used to the idea."

Narrowing her eyes and speaking slowly, as if to a half-wit, Kerry said, "I don't want to get involved."

"It's too late to worry about that." He grazed her cheek with his knuckles. "I want you, Kerry."

"Well, you can't have me."

"I usually manage to get what I want." The pleasure and passion had left her eyes, he noted. They were now sparkling with sheer irritation. He moved closer, enjoying himself.

"Not this time, hotshot."

He grinned. "You were going to tell me about your vacation."

Kerry eyed him warily, then gave a small shrug, relieved at the reprieve. Moving back a little, she said, "It was...uneventful." Lonely, actually, at times. "I spent most of the time on Oahu, doing the usual tourist stuff. Flew to Kauai for a couple of days."

"No one bothered you?"

She shook her head. "I rented a car, traveled around the islands, went to a couple of luaus, saw all the sights and took a jillion pictures."

"Of what?"

"A bit of everything." She shrugged. "It's a hobby I don't always take time to enjoy, so I went after the perfect sunset and got distracted by birds, flowers and local people. Anything that looked interesting."

"Can I see them?"

"You'll be bored silly, but sure. When I get them back. I dropped them in a photo shop the day I hit town and haven't picked them up yet."

"And nothing happened—besides your room being tossed—to upset you during those two weeks?"

She stared out the window, thinking. Remembering. Shaking her head, she said decisively, "Nothing. You're barking up the wrong tree, Devin. My life is an open book. And—" she stared down at the stacks of sheets, thinking of the work ahead of her "—right now it's one of all work and no play."

Devin reached out and touched a tendril of hair, wrapping it around his finger. "Well, we'll just have to work on that, won't we?"

Five

—

Oh, yeah, Devin thought four days later, watching Kerry stand at the front door with a clipboard, checking the furniture being carried in by several of his cousins. He really did have to work on her. In the past few days she had hardly stopped long enough to breathe, much less relax and sit down. Especially anywhere near him. Or even in the same room.

Not that he was surprised. Kerry was definitely skittish. Gun-shy. Running as fast as she could. Anywhere, as long as it was away from him.

"Hey, Dev."

Devin lifted a hand in greeting. "Tom. How's it going?" Another cousin, with the bronzed skin and dark hair of an islander. He was giving a hand with the heavy antiques Megan and Kerry had selected from the warehouse.

"Be just fine when you introduce me to the cute little *malihini.*"

Tucking his hands into the back pockets of his jeans, Devin narrowed his eyes. "You know her name. That's enough. Just remember she's your boss today, not a newcomer or a tourist, and you'll do just fine."

Tom's easy smile broadened to a grin. "Are we a bit touchy here? You're not going to brag about me a little? No telling her I'm the island surfing champ? I give lessons, you know." He shot another glance toward the house. "Cheap. Maybe even free."

"Don't even think about it." Anything Kerry wanted to learn about the island, she could damn well learn from him. Including surfing. Especially surfing.

"You serious?" Tom tilted his head, waiting.

"Yeah."

Tom blinked. "You *are* serious. Is this the family's most determined bachelor talking?"

"She's taken," Devin said flatly. "Just so there's no mistake, I'll tell you how the rest of the day's going to go for you. Nowhere, with her. You're going to bust your butt hauling furniture. And for that, you get Megan's thanks and maybe a couple of beers. Then you climb in the truck and take off. And you don't come back."

Tom's dark eyes gleamed with amusement. "Whatever happened to island hospitality?" he murmured. "Aunt Mei would be shocked. She raised up her boy better than that."

"She gave up on a few lessons. I never learned to share worth a damn."

"Does the lady feel the same way?"

"Don't worry about it." Devin's voice roughened with a flick of temper that surprised him as much as it did his cousin. "If she doesn't now, she will. Soon."

"Dev, old buddy, I hate to say it, but you're getting testy in your old age." He looked around when a shrill whistle came from the direction of the truck. "Better get back to earning my beer allotment. See you later."

"Not here."

Tom grinned. "At your folks' house. This Saturday. The monthly gathering of the clan. You going to bring the pretty *malihini?*"

"Yeah." If he could drag her away from the house for a few hours.

Turning her loose at a family gathering was a risk, in a lot of ways. But, what the hell. He gave a philosophic shrug. Life was a risk. Besides, his relatives had more to do than sit around discussing their latest psychic breakthroughs.

Of course, there was always the hurdle of his mother. Mei had a sixth sense that was downright spooky. It was said she could take one look at a man and woman and know if the intangible spark existed that would transform them into a couple. A serious couple—as in marriage. He wasn't sure he believed it, but he knew for sure that not one damn thing escaped her eagle eyes. In this case, he had a gut feeling she'd see a man who wanted a woman more than he should and a woman running as fast as she could.

As for the rest of them, as long as no one brought up his link with Megan, he'd be fine. If the matter did come up, he'd do what he always did. Play it by ear.

He'd been doing that most of his life—starting on his first day of school. It hadn't taken him long to figure out that teachers weren't happy when someone tiptoed through their minds. It had been like living a double life, or working undercover, but he'd managed. And lately, since the day he'd walked in on Kerry, he'd honed the skill to a fine art.

She wasn't stupid. Nor was she by nature a suspicious person. But after he'd jumped all over her a couple of times, demanding answers before she'd known for sure she had a problem, she had become a tad testy. He grinned, remembering her nicely pointed statement about not having had a keeper since she'd left for college. Her unspoken message had been loud and clear—butt out, Murphy. I'm a big girl.

He knew exactly what she was, and that's what was driving him crazy. Ambling toward the house—toward Kerry—he watched her check off an item on her list and direct Tom to the living room. His pace quickened when his cousin hesitated, smiling down at her.

She wasn't wearing shorts today, he noted. Instead—and probably with deliberation, knowing the house would be crawling with a truckful of movers—she had chosen tan jeans and a creamy cotton sweater. Probably her idea of conservative, hormone-quelling work clothes. He grinned at the thought. Someday he'd tell her exactly what those hip-hugging pants did to his blood pressure. Her hair was just the way he liked it, too, sliding out of the untidy bun atop her head, silky tendrils touching her nape.

But she was all business today, he noted with satisfaction, slowing down again. She merely gave Tom an absent smile and pointed her pencil toward the other room.

He took the porch stairs two at a time. "Everything okay?"

Kerry looked up at him, suppressed excitement gleaming in her eyes. "It's starting to fall into place," she said sedately.

Devin gazed at her vivid face. She was in her element, he thought. Making a home, imprinting the place with her special brand of magic. Enthusiasm colored every check mark she made on her list, eagerness poured out of her and seeped into him.

Even if he hadn't felt it, he would have recognized the look of delight. She'd had it yesterday when a truckload of rugs had been delivered. As far as he was concerned, a carpet was simply something that covered the floor, nothing to get excited about. But after she'd spent the day arranging them to her own satisfaction, she'd taken him from room to room, pointing out the merits of each one. Most of them were Orientals—area rugs, enhancing the gleaming, broadplanked floors—that were as enduring as they were beautiful.

And she had been so damned excited, already visualizing what each room would look like when furnished. The same elation was pouring through her now, growing with each piece of furniture carried through the door.

"You like this old stuff, don't you?"

She nodded, watching anxiously as a large buffet was levered out of the back of the truck by three swearing, sweating men. "Doesn't everyone?"

He made a noncommittal noise, thinking of the functional stainless steel and leather furniture in his condo. "What are you doing Saturday night?" he asked abruptly. Something moved in his chest when she shot him a wary glance. He didn't want her too comfortable around him, didn't want her thinking of him as a buddy or a brother. So, for now, that edgy, cautious look suited him just fine.

"It depends," she said dryly after a moment, keeping her gaze pinned on the truck. "What *part* of the night? Are you thinking of feeding me or trying to get me into bed?"

"Both." He grinned when she blinked up at him, momentarily forgetting her precious buffet. "We'll start with a well-chaperoned meal and take it from there."

Kerry's brows rose. "I think I can manage dinner without help. Where?"

"At my folks' place. With a lot of other people. Once a month they have the family over for a big potluck. I'd like you to come."

She hesitated. "If it's family, maybe I shouldn't—"

"You won't. You'll enjoy it—unless you don't like crowds."

Kerry grinned. "An innkeeper who doesn't like people? Get real, Murphy."

"Fine. It's settled. Seven okay?" At her nod, he added, "Dress casual. It's not a fancy affair."

"What can I bring?"

"Just yourself. I'll take care of the rest."

"Are you sure it's just family in there?" They stood on the lighted path leading to the backyard, and Kerry rested her hand on Devin's arm, stopping him. She tilted her head, listening to the buzz of voices, the laughter coming from the other side of the high wooden gate.

"Yeah. If you think this is bad, wait till you see them." Devin kept his smile casual, wondering how many of his cousins he'd have to dump in the pool before the night was over. Kerry's idea of casual had pushed up his temperature several notches. She was wearing a pale yellow sundress that left her shoulders bare and seemed to be held up by one thin strap around her neck. Bare legs and thonged sandals with small narrow heels completed the outfit. His hand tightened on the latch. "Ready?"

"Ready."

Devin threw open the gate and looked down at Kerry. He knew what was inside and was more interested in her reaction. She didn't disappoint him. Her eyes widened in disbelief as she gazed at the jumble of genes milling around. They covered the spectrum from blondes to redheads to dark-eyed, bronzed islanders.

"My God. It's half the town."

"Nah. Just seems that way." And it might be a bit overwhelming to Kerry, who had grown up with no brothers or sisters.

"How many?" she demanded in delight. "Just give me a ballpark figure."

Devin shrugged. "I lost count several years ago. When they were in their twenties, my father and his two brothers left Ireland and settled here. Each of them had large families, eighteen kids in all. Now most of them have married and have families of their own." He gave her a wicked grin. "You can do some real wheeling and dealing tonight. Most of the cousins on Joanie's list are here."

"I expect introductions to all of them. Oh, Devin, the yard," she said reverently. "Just look at it."

Obediently, Devin looked, trying to see it through her eyes. It was a big chunk of property, and the house had been remodeled in stages, as the family had grown. It was actually more of a compound than a single structure. An open-air patio extended from the house and led in a meandering way back to the swimming pool. A walk wound past gardens of tropical plants to several guest cottages. Much of the complex had been built on the island plan, using screens instead of walls so they could take advantage of the trade winds and sunlight. Back beyond the pool was a large combination office and master bedroom his father had built years ago so he and Mei could occasionally escape from their boisterous family.

But it was the yard that fascinated Kerry. He linked his fingers through hers and led her down a twisting pathway past miniature waterfalls, cascading fountains, ponds and lacy ferns. White fairy lights blinked in some of the trees, highlighting white rattan furniture with fat, colorful cushions that provided bright conversational areas.

Devin stopped near the pool, taking pleasure in Kerry's unabashed delight. He ran his thumb over her knuckles, enjoying the feel of her slim fingers laced with his, her slim body brushing against him.

"It's unbelievable." Kerry turned to take it all in. "So much to see."

"Most of it's my dad's work." Devin grinned. "He tends to get carried away."

"It's perfect. I wouldn't change a thing."

"Ah, a woman of sound judgment and even better taste. Maybe there's hope for my son, after all."

Kerry turned at the sound of the deep voice and found herself facing a striking couple.

Devin tugged Kerry closer, his hand settling at her waist. "Mom, Dad, this is Kerry Cottrell, Megan and Luke's new magician at Rainbow's End. Kerry, my parents, Sean and Mei."

Kerry blinked, looking from father to son as Devin hugged his mother, and knew exactly what Devin would look like in another thirty years.

Devastating.

Sexy.

With a touch of something untamed in his blue eyes.

Sean was a redheaded giant, whose flaming hair was softened by a sheen of gray. He looked hard enough to crack coconuts in his bare hands but visibly softened when he looked down at the slim, dark-eyed woman at his side.

Mei had black hair barely touched with silver, a slow smile, and the serene beauty and strength needed to tame a turbulent Celt.

Sean, as Kerry suspected he always did, got the first word in. Ignoring his son, he beamed at Kerry and confiscated her free hand. Lifting it, he brushed his lips across her fingers. Kerry smiled, utterly charmed. "Megan told us she found a miracle worker to take over the place. She didn't mention you were a raving beauty. Is my boy taking good care of you?"

Kerry retrieved her hand, slanting a wry look at Devin. "Don't encourage him. If it was left up to Devin, Rainbow's End would be surrounded by a high fence topped with broken glass."

Sean scowled. "Not a bad idea when people are sneaking around leaving footprints all over the place."

"*Aloha*, Kerry. Welcome to our house," Mei said serenely, touching Kerry's arm with slim fingers. They tightened fractionally for an instant, and Kerry blinked at the intent dark eyes studying her.

"Thank you. You have a beautiful home."

"You'll come back to enjoy it." Mei's smile was slow and warm. "Often." Her calm gaze switched to her son. "Devin, introduce Kerry to everyone. Make sure she meets Uncle Loe."

Devin and Sean's blue eyes met in a purely masculine exchange. They knew that tone of voice. Mei's antenna was definitely up.

"Yeah, I'll do that."

As he turned away, taking Kerry with him, Devin remembered why he never brought dates to these affairs. He had seen his mother in action too many times and had decided early on that he didn't want that kind of interference in his life. It was hard enough dealing with his own psychic reactions without having Mei's instincts battering at him.

There was a flurry of sound, and Devin looked up just as Megan hurled herself at him. "Hey, little brother. I never see you anymore."

He caught her and gave her a quick hug, looking down at her radiant face. "You're keeping me busy, that's why. You look good, Sunshine. Luke must be treating you well."

Her grin traveled from her brother to her husband. "He'll do in a pinch." Luke, tall, dark-eyed and patient, retrieved his wife and tucked her under his arm.

Kerry watched the byplay. It was the first time she had seen Megan and Devin together. They were definitely twins, with all the closeness she had expected, but there was something more, something she couldn't put her finger on. A silent communication that seemed to say more than mere words.

Megan stretched up to give Luke a swift kiss. "There's a lot of people here I want Kerry to meet. You two entertain yourselves for a while, okay?" When he nodded, she grabbed Kerry's hand. "Come on. Let's make the rounds." Looking over her shoulder, she grinned at Devin. "I'll keep the wolves away, little brother."

When the women disappeared into the crowd and the two men were alone, Luke turned to Devin. "How are things going?"

"At the house?"

"Let's start with you. I have to get the latest dirt for Megan. I'm curious, what did Mei just say to you?"

"Why?"

"My mother-in-law's mind fascinates me. When Megan first introduced us, I was in the early stage of lust, but Mei saw wedding bells."

Devin's thoughts drifted to Kerry, wondering if he should go after her. He could introduce her as well as Megan. And he'd be a lot more selective. "She told me to make sure Kerry met Uncle Loe," he said absently.

"Well, since he's the man who does all the family weddings, I guess we know what she's thinking. Is she always right?"

"No." Just often enough to make people edgy when she got that look in her eyes.

Luke put his hand on Devin's shoulder, briefly tightening his grip. "Either way, it doesn't make things any easier."

"I'm not thinking of marriage," Devin said flatly.

"Well, Uncle Loe does the blessings, too, so Kerry will be coordinating things with him. Maybe that's what she meant."

Devin frowned at the space where he had last seen Kerry. "She doesn't like psychics," he said abruptly. "Doesn't believe in them. Thinks they're weird."

"Welcome to the club," Luke murmured. "That's just about where I was nine months ago. Have you told her? About you? The family?"

"Hell, no. Do you think I'm crazy?"

Luke gazed at him thoughtfully. "You brought her here tonight, right into the lion's den. I'm not sure."

"She'll be okay. But you and Megan see a lot of her, and I'd . . . rather you didn't let anything slip. I'll tell her myself."

"When?"

Devin shrugged. "When the time is right." When she trusts me. When she won't be afraid. Or furious.

"Okay. It's your neck." Luke frowned, then said brusquely, "In the meantime, she's here on her own, at our request, with no family. What—"

"Luke, you're not asking me what my intentions are, are you?" Devin's gaze was cool.

"I'm just—"

"Don't. Kerry's twenty-seven and I'm even older. We're both single. Whatever happens between us is our business."

Luke swore softly. "You're right. Let's move on before I get my foot so far in my mouth I can't get it out. What about the house?"

"It's finished. Wired. I'm having a hell of a time with Kerry, though. About the system. She says a bed and breakfast shouldn't be locked up like a jail." His gaze met Luke's. "And I've found several sets of prints on the grounds in the last few days. Different ones."

"Well, hell."

"Yeah. My feeling exactly."

Luke walked over to a nearby cooler and snagged two beers. When he handed one to Devin, he asked, "Are you sure they weren't there before?"

Devin took a long swallow before he replied. "They're fresh."

"So what are you going to do?"

"Keep watching. Hope he gets careless. He set off the silent alarm the first night it was installed, but he was gone by the time I got outside."

Luke's brows rose. "Did you tell Kerry?"

Devin shook his head. "No. She's got enough on her mind these days. As long as I'm around, it's one less thing for her to worry about."

The two of them began walking down the winding path, oblivious to the crowd around them. "You don't think she should be told?"

Devin gave him a level look. "I'm there, you're not. It's my call."

"Okay." Luke shrugged. "Have any idea who's doing it?"

"No. Not a one. I've decided that whoever it is, he's more a nuisance than a threat. There's been no damage since the windows that first night."

"What about Kerry's car window?"

Devin dodged two of his nephews who called out an apology and cannonballed into the pool. "I think it was an accident. Chalk it up to inexperience or carelessness, but I don't think it was deliberate."

"Why not?"

"It's the damnedest thing," Devin said, running a hand through his hair. "A couple of days after it happened, Kerry got a letter. An envelope, actually. No note, no explanation. Just enough money to cover the cost of fixing the window."

"A crook with a conscience?"

"Looks like it."

"Damned strange," Luke agreed. "And you still don't have any idea why he keeps coming back?"

"No. Kerry's so clean she squeaks. And there's been nothing in the house worth stealing. But he'll do it once too often, and I'll get him."

"And when you do?"

Devin shrugged. "We'll see."

Luke finished his beer and held out his hand for Devin's empty can. Dumping them both in a plastic trash bag, he said, "Dev?"

"Mmm?"

"Megan thinks you might not be linked up with her anymore. What do you think?"

"Hell, I don't know. Things have been pretty quiet on that front lately. Maybe you've been keeping her out of trouble. Or maybe I've just been so damned busy reacting to Kerry, I haven't had time to listen."

Luke grinned. "What's been happening?"

"What hasn't? I'm losing a hell of a lot of sleep, for one thing. Kerry's a night owl, wanders around the place at all hours when she can't sleep. I wake up with my heart pounding, go to see what's the matter and find her scared to death because a spider's on the wall or a field mouse is running across the floor."

Luke's crack of laughter drew sympathetic grins from a handful of teenagers. "And what does she think when you keep coming to the rescue?"

"Damned if I know," Devin said with a rueful grin. "At that time of night there aren't too many good excuses around. I usually tell her I'm on my way to the kitchen or the bathroom. She probably thinks I have the biggest thirst and the weakest bladder on the island."

"Well, it doesn't sound dull, anyway. What about the business angle? Can you work from the house?"

"Computers are amazing things. You'd be surprised how much information I can gather without ever leaving my desk. I'm delegating more than I used to, but it's working. And if I have to be gone, I have one of the guys sit in for me."

"So you'll stay?"

Devin nodded. "Until the place opens and there are guests. I'd do it even if you weren't paying expenses."

"It's my place, my responsibility," Luke said with a shrug. "By the way, come by sometime and see the latest addition to the family. I bought Megan a pup. Eventually, it's supposed to be a watchdog, but all it's doing so far is tearing up the house."

"Keep an eye on it," Devin advised. "Someone just took one of my clients for a bundle. Ransom for her pet poodle."

Luke's brows rose. "And got away with it?"

"I'm working on it," Devin said laconically.

Across the yard, the two women claimed a secluded wicker sofa. After a few moments, Kerry looked at Megan. "Your family does this every month?"

Megan grinned. "Gruesome thought, huh?"

"No! I think it's wonderful."

"The great thing about this—" Megan's airy wave included the entire setting "—is that we're all here because we want to be." Changing the subject abruptly, she said, "You look like you have something on your mind. Are things moving along all right at Rainbow's End?"

"Yeah. Everything's on or ahead of schedule so far."

"But?"

Kerry scowled at the enormous fern next to her, reaching out to touch a curling frond. "It's this damned security. I can't live in a house that bristles with dead bolts and alarms. And what about the guests? They'll wander in and out at all hours. I can't impose a curfew on them, for heaven's sake."

"You're absolutely right." Megan's voice was soothing. Security wasn't the only thing bothering Kerry, she knew. It simply made a more acceptable point of complaint, far better than the real problem—Megan's own charming and arrogant twin.

"This is only temporary, I promise. I'm afraid we all overreacted when someone messed with the dining room windows. I've lived here all my life, and it never occurred to me that you might not be safe out there. Devin pointed it out in no uncertain terms."

"He would," Kerry muttered. "What is it about me that makes everyone think I need a keeper?"

"Just men," Megan corrected. "Their protective instincts go into overdrive when they deal with small, attractive women. If I had thought that, you wouldn't be here now."

"Thanks."

"Anyway," Megan continued, "we had ordered an ordinary, ho-hum kind of security. Devin insisted we upgrade it."

"He would."

"You can't fault him," Megan said thoughtfully. "He's seen some pretty grim things at places that weren't protected. So now you have the top-of-the-line stuff, guaranteed to flash lights and ring bells and whistles if any bad guys show up."

"But—"

Megan held up her hand. "Let me finish. It may be necessary now, while you're there alone." She shrugged. "I don't know. Devin thinks it is. But as soon as the first guests arrive—and my fussbudget brother leaves—we'll call the company and have them adapt it to as little or as much as you're comfortable with. As far as I'm concerned, all we need is enough to satisfy the insurance requirements."

"And Luke?" Kerry asked delicately. "Does he agree with you?"

Megan chuckled and patted Kerry on the shoulder. "Absolutely. As long as you're safe. Remember, my husband's in the hotel business. He's not about to chase away guests. He'd rather pay higher insurance premiums." She studied Kerry's relieved expression. "So, can you live with this until the opening?"

Kerry nodded. "I can hold my breath for that long."

"Good. Now, have we talked about the blessing?"

"The what?" Kerry looked at her blankly.

"Darn." Megan ran a hand through her hair. "I knew I'd forgotten something. I hate to drop this on you, but it has to be done. Probably a day or so before the grand opening. Of course, we can do it on opening day, but I think adding several hundred people to the first day is just asking for trouble, don't you?"

"Several hundred—" Kerry cleared her throat and started again. "Exactly what *is* this blessing thing?"

Megan leaned back and contemplated the leafy branches overhead. "An island tradition," she finally said. "It's expected. Sort of a house warming with religious overtones. Whenever someone moves into a new house or opens a business, they have one."

Her blue eyes met Kerry's. "It's very important to the people here."

Kerry waited several moments, then let out a long breath, hoping it didn't sound like a sigh. "Then we'll do it. *Before* the opening. We'll have refreshments, I suppose?"

"Definitely," Megan said cheerfully. "We shoot the works. Drinks, desserts, lots of *pupus.*"

"Poo-poos?"

"Island hors d'oeuvres, snacks, whatever. Call our cousin Tony—he has a catering service—and just tell him how many people you expect. He'll take care of it. His crew also does setup and cleanup, so you won't have to worry about that."

"And how many *do* we expect?" Kerry asked carefully.

"Well, we start with the family and go from there. Say four hundred, tops. We'll need a lot of folding chairs, I suppose." She laughed when Kerry closed her eyes and sighed. "You're going to hate me before we even get open. Listen, I know someone who owns a calligraphy shop. We'll get her to do the invitations."

Kerry opened her eyes. "A cousin?"

"What else?" Megan jumped to her feet. "Come on, we'd better hustle or my mother will be popping out from behind a bush asking who you've met. If you tell her no one, I'm in big trouble."

Following obediently, Kerry said, "Your mother said I was to meet your uncle Loe."

"Uncle Loe?" Megan stopped, gazing at her thoughtfully.

"Did I get the name wrong? I thought that was what she said."

"No, you got it right." Megan turned away, hiding her grin. She wondered if her brother's bachelor stomach was still churning. Mei's little comments often had that effect. "Uncle Loe does all the local blessings," she said casually. "But I'll let Devin take you to him."

"Oh." Kerry followed along. "Megan?"

"Mmm?"

"There isn't anything else you forgot to tell me, is there?"

Six

An hour later Kerry had found cousin Tony and was engaged in an animated discussion about folding chairs. Four hundred of them, to be exact.

"Tables *and* chairs, set beneath the banyan tree," she was insisting when a hard arm slid around her waist. It drew her back to an even harder body. Devin. She felt a shiver race along her skin, her blood scramble through her veins. She also saw Tony's slow grin as he glanced at the two of them, and it annoyed the hell out of her.

She took a deep, slow breath and released it. He was picking up the pace, she fretted. Moving in. Fast. She was going to have to do something about him. And she would, she promised. Later. Giving Devin's hand a deliberately casual pat, she held Tony's dark gaze and said, "Linens. Pink, I think. With white candles. And flowers, maybe floating."

Pursing his lips in a soundless whistle, Tony slid his hands into the pockets of his shorts and rocked back on his heels. "You're talking big bucks here. Planning to break the McCall bank?"

"Just denting it a little. I cleared it with Luke. It's called advertising expenses."

Devin's fingers tightened at her waist in a none too subtle reminder that he was still there. "She'll get bids from the competition," he warned lazily.

Tony's quick laugh cut the leaping tension. "Hell, man, there ain't no such animal on the island. I'm the only one big enough to handle it." His gaze switched back to Kerry. "So we're going first-class?"

She nodded. "Always. Think old-fashioned, casual elegance. I want the affair to reflect the house. I'll call you tomorrow with a date."

"Which you can't set until you talk with Uncle Loe," Devin said smoothly, "so I suggest we find him. Tony, maybe you should catch up with your wife before she decides she just might get along without you."

Tony glanced at his watch and swore. "She's going to kill me."

"Not if she's the one who has the calligraphy shop." Kerry pointed behind him. "She's holed up with Megan, talking guest lists." When Devin nudged her in the opposite direction, she waved a hasty farewell.

"Having fun?" he asked, leading her down a lighted path toward a slim man with a shock of gray hair.

"Yeah. Do you suppose someone in the family would like to adopt me?" She broke off as a toddler darted toward them. When he plopped down at their feet, Kerry scooped him up, laughing softly at his gleeful grin. "This kid's going to give his folks a run for their money."

"Right now, I think it's his sister who's doing the running. Over here, Sara," he called to an anxious ten-year-old who was peering behind a huge fern. "We've got him."

After Kerry turned her squirming bundle over to a relieved and indignant Sara, she looked up at Devin. "You guys do this every month?"

"Like clockwork. Every fourth Saturday. Are you wondering how we do it without killing each other off?"

"No." Kerry shifted her gaze back to the path. "I'm envying you. Our family gatherings take place in my folks' dining room and the four of us don't take up much space around the table."

Devin's hand tightened around hers. "Well, before we talk about an adoption, we have to get through a blessing. And here's the man who can deal with both of them. Uncle Loe, I want you to meet Kerry Cottrell."

Were all the men in this family drop-dead gorgeous? Kerry wondered when the older man turned to greet her. Slim, with bronzed skin and gray curly hair, his face was lean, creased by time and weather, his dark, kind eyes gleaming with serene wisdom.

"No need to be formal," Loe said, stepping forward and giving her a gentle hug. "I've heard many things about Kerry. All good." He smiled at her. "*Aloha*, Kerry. Thank you for bringing life to Rainbow's End again. It's a new beginning for the old place—one that will reflect your own sense of joy. Rainbow's End will become a place of refuge for your many guests."

"Thank you." She blinked, touched by words that sounded almost prophetic, as well as by his manner. She still didn't understand exactly what a blessing was, but if this man performed the ceremony, she was willing to bet it would be a humdinger.

Almost as if he could read her thoughts, he said, "Now, we plan the blessing, no?"

Kerry grinned. "We plan the blessing, yes. What do we do first?"

"Set the date."

They both pulled out small notebooks, consulted calendars and each other, and penciled in a date and time.

"Now what?" Kerry asked.

The older man shrugged. "I perform the ceremony and you take care of the festivities. They can be as simple or elaborate as you like."

"That's it?"

He nodded. "I don't know how to make it any more complicated."

"I don't really understand what a blessing is," Kerry admitted, wishing she'd had time to look into the matter before discussing it with the man who played the major role.

Loe smiled. "You're new to our ways. No reason you should. But I'll be happy to explain it. Anytime."

He was a kind man, and gentle, she thought, realizing he had selected the words carefully. His eyes were caring, understanding. But she suspected that not far beneath the surface lay a reservoir, a depth that when called upon made him a man of formidable strength.

"Are you a minister?" she asked suddenly.

His smile broadened to a grin. "Among other things. And if there's anything else I can do for you—" he looked from her to Devin and back again "—in any capacity, it will be my pleasure."

"Thanks, but I think that'll do it for now, Uncle Loe," Devin said blandly, dropping his hand to Kerry's waist and nudging her forward. "Kerry, I think I hear the food being set up. Are you hungry?"

It was well after midnight when they got in Devin's BMW and headed for home. Kerry leaned back and lowered the window, enjoying the balmy breeze tossing her hair. Sliding off her sandals and digging her toes in the carpet, she thought about Devin's family. A real Mulligan stew—with a copious amount of island spices thrown in for good measure. Boisterous, caring, with a genuine reverence for the older generations.

Mei was the perfect matriarch for the clan. Calm and serene, the ideal mate for her tempestuous Celt. Her tranquil gaze didn't miss a thing, either. In fact, if she were inclined to be fanciful, Kerry thought, it would be easy to believe that Mei's gaze bored through the surface straight to the heart and soul. If she believed in mind readers, she would consider Mei a good candidate.

Shifting her gaze to Devin, she studied the son. He drove as competently as he did everything, she reflected, watching his hands on the steering wheel. His fingers were long, his palms broad, and they moved on the wheel as if he didn't have a nerve in his body. He was a man who accomplished a great deal with very little fuss, she thought, blinking at the realization.

Actually, the only time she'd seen him show any signs of stress was when he was yelling at her. And that, she thought darkly, was happening all too often these days. Although why he should get so upset when she saw a spider was beyond her. Well, she decided fatalistically, if that was a problem for him, he'd better not be around if she ever spotted a cockroach.

He was an unusual man, no doubt about it.

He was also a man who was beginning to make her nervous. Very, very nervous.

How did these things happen to her? she wondered in exasperation. She had left two troublesome men behind, quit a job and crossed an ocean, all to simplify her life. And what did she have to show for the effort?

A sexy, self-appointed guardian.

A man who crowded her.

A man who wanted her.

A man who had spent the evening being openly possessive in front of his entire family.

It was all a bit much for a woman who planned to concentrate exclusively on her career. A woman who had apparently made some serious mistakes dealing with two average, inoffensive men. A woman who didn't know the first thing about handling a man like Devin Murphy.

Uncomfortable with her thoughts and the silence they had produced, she shifted and said lightly, "I like your family."

"So do I."

Aided by the dim light of the dashboard, she saw his grin. "Especially your uncle Loe," she persevered.

"Most people feel that way."

"Is he really a minister?"

Devin slanted her a look. "He said he was, didn't he?"

"He also said 'among other things,'" she reminded him. "What does that mean?"

"That he's a *kahuna*." He waited, wondering what her reaction would be. Over the years, he'd seen enough of them to know it could range from a blank, questioning stare to outright distaste. When it came, he almost laughed. She was game, but she didn't have a clue.

"Right. A *kahuna*." She gazed at his profile for a few moments, then sighed. "All right, I give. Is that good or bad?"

"Take your choice," Devin said with a shrug. "Even here on the islands, people disagree. Some call him a holy man, some a priest. Others say he's a shaman. Still others refer to him as a—"

"Oh, my God," she said in an appalled voice. "A witch doctor. Not that nice man. Tell me you're kidding."

"I'm kidding," Devin said obediently.

Kerry winced. "Could you say it with a little more conviction, please? Just say it isn't so."

"If you're thinking of him in terms of someone who cuts off chicken heads and sticks pins in voodoo dolls, it definitely isn't so. Other than that, it isn't so easy to define. Uncle Loe doesn't care what people call him. He does a lot of good for the people here, and that's the important thing. He has a few detractors, but he's an important man in our community."

Devin drove silently through the dark night, giving her time to absorb what he'd said, wondering what thoughts were going on behind that pensive expression. When he'd just about decided she wasn't going to commit herself, Kerry shifted, turning to face him.

"I don't care what some people think," she said militantly. "That man would never do anything wrong. He couldn't."

And that, Devin thought with a grin, was apparently that. Kerry had given it a whole ten seconds of thought and chosen sides. He rested his hand on her thigh, squeezing gently. "That's my girl," he said approvingly. "Join Uncle Loe's fan club. To hell with logic, your sentiments are in the right place." His grin broadened when she picked up his hand and put it back on the steering wheel.

"Drive," she said firmly.

He drove, taking pleasure in the soft night air, the smooth movement of the BMW, the presence of the woman beside him. The scent of wildflowers drifted toward him, making his stomach tighten. Making more than that tighten, he admitted to himself. Since the first time he'd seen her, he had been walking around in a state of half arousal, and it was getting damned tiresome.

The silence in the car wasn't broken until after he'd pulled into the garage. He walked around to Kerry's side just as she slid out.

"Hold on," he said calmly as she tried to eel her way around him. Sliding his arm around her waist to keep her close, he shortened his step to match hers as they followed the path to the house. When they reached the front porch, the sensor-activated light snapped on and Kerry began scrabbling for her key.

"Slow down," Devin advised, watching her shove things aside in her small straw bag. "You'll dump that stuff all over the porch. Are we in a hurry?"

Kerry gave him a frazzled look. "No! Not at all," she said, lying through her teeth. No hurry at all. Just a matter of survival, of getting through the door before something happened that they'd both regret.

"Good. Because now that we have both the blessing and Uncle Loe settled, I'd like to talk about us."

Shock jolted through her. It wasn't as if she hadn't expected it, Kerry reminded herself, willing her hands to stop their frantic searching. After all, Devin *was* big on talking things out. Anyone with a sliver of perception would have seen it coming. She'd just hoped it could be put off for a reasonable time. Say, a year or so.

"Us?" she asked cautiously. When he just raised his brows and slanted a look at her, Kerry sighed. He wasn't going to make this easy.

Knowing she had to take a stand before things got completely out of hand, she said firmly, "The way I see it, there is no us. What we have here are two individuals forced by unusual circumstances to occupy the same house. The *house*," she emphasized. "Not the same bed or even the same room."

"I'm hoping to change that," Devin murmured. "Real soon."

"Therefore," she declared, doing her best to ignore him, "while I hate to beat a dead horse, I'll say it again. There is no us."

His gaze dropped to her mouth, lingered. He smiled when she nervously touched her tongue to her bottom lip.

"It won't work, sweetheart."

Kerry's hands stilled. "What won't?"

"You can't talk it away."

She stared at him stubbornly, wiggling a finger in her bag, trying to snag her keys. All she needed was a couple of seconds, she reasoned. Just time enough to open the door and hightail it to her room. "Talk what away?" She stalled, her finger touching cold metal. "And don't call me sweetheart."

"This." Devin tossed her bag onto the wooden swing and wrapped his hands around her waist. When he leaned back against the porch rail, he took her with him, easing his grip when she stopped right where he wanted her—in the space between his spread thighs, pressing against him.

"Devin!" Kerry braced her hands on his broad shoulders and fought the impulse to let them slide around his neck. Tempting as the idea was, it would not be a smart thing to do. In fact, it would be down-right stupid. A bad idea. This was a man who, given an inch, would take a country mile. A man who had the notion that what he wanted was his for the taking—and what he wanted right now was her.

The fact that she was tempted was simply a case of temporary insanity, Kerry assured herself. Or a death wish. If she was going to survive this ridiculous situation—unscathed—until the guests arrived, she had to keep her wits about her. And her distance.

Kerry stiffened her arms and shoved. It was like pushing a rock. She tried again, putting more muscle into it—and didn't have any more luck than she'd had the first time.

"Devin, this isn't funny. Let me go."

"I don't think I can," he said slowly. "Not this time, honey. I want you. I have since the first day I walked in here."

"Bolted in," she said breathlessly.

"Whatever."

"Gun drawn and looking for trouble."

"Well, I found it, didn't I?" His arms tightened around her waist, drawing her deeper into his heat, against the hard flesh pressing against his zipper.

Kerry took a shaky breath. They were too close, bodies brushing, heat swirling around them. Her face was level with his, and what she saw in his blue eyes made her more nervous than ever. Lazy sensuality stirred, coupled with a hunger he didn't try to hide.

Devin lifted a hand, but before she could sigh with relief, he buried it in her hair. He ignored the pins that dropped, concentrating on shaping her head with his fingers. His grip was firm, determined.

Kerry arched into his touch, murmuring a soft sound of approval. That was all he needed. She didn't have time to protest or refuse. His mouth was on hers, covering, pleasuring, taking, giving.

She felt the jolt all the way to her toes. He wasn't going to stop, she realized hazily. He would push until her back was to the wall. Until she said yes. Or at least until she stopped saying no. Kerry slid her arms around his neck, a wave of wild alarm washing over her. It was followed by unutterable relief.

"This isn't smart." But even as she whispered the words, her fingers tangled in his hair.

"Mmm." Devin brushed his lips at the corner of her eye.

"It's just . . . chemistry."

"Let's hear it for chemistry," he murmured lazily, nipping her earlobe, smiling when she shuddered.

"I really don't want to get involved." Kerry's mouth turned toward his.

"You already are."

He was right. She was. It wasn't the right time or place for her—and not the type of man she had expected. But he was the man who made her pulse go haywire. The man who created such a hunger in her, her soul trembled.

When he lifted his mouth from hers, they were both breathless. Shaken. Wanting more.

"I'll tell you how it is, sweetheart," Devin muttered near her ear, sliding his hands down her back, lingering on the soft fullness of her bottom. "If you say no, right now, you get to walk through the door and head upstairs to your room."

Kerry stilled, blinking at his shoulder. "And if I don't?"

His fingers flexed, bringing her closer. "We go through it together, to my room. And we don't come out till morning." Waiting, he wondered if his heart would pound out of his chest.

"Devin, I—"

"Yes or no?" Instinctively, his hands tightened.

Kerry rested her brow against his shoulder. "Yes."

"What?" Devin barely breathed, need tearing through him, the roar of blood so loud in his head he couldn't hear her.

"Yes," Kerry mumbled a bit louder.

"Yes?"

She reared back in exasperation to glare at him. What did he want her to do? Notify the neighbors? *"Yes!"*

As she watched, the look of taut control in his blue eyes changed. Relief first, then a blaze of triumph. He scooped her up and stopped at the swing, allowing her to grab her straw bag.

"Open the door." He waited impatiently while she pulled out the key and inserted it in the lock. Stepping inside, he kicked the door shut behind him and didn't stop until he reached his room.

Devin dropped Kerry lightly on the large bed and reached out to the small lamp on the dresser. When she blinked in the sudden light, he gazed down at her a long, tense moment.

Dropping down beside her, Devin planted a hand on either side of her head, looking down into hazel eyes that were wide with wonder and a tinge of doubt.

"You're not changing your mind, are you?" His voice was rough, but his fingers were gentle in her hair. If he saw as much as a trace of fear, he would let her go, even if it sliced him in two. But when she shifted and stroked her cheek against his wrist, his heart bounced and he let out a long breath he hadn't been aware of holding.

Because she found it hard to breathe, Kerry's voice was almost a whisper. "No. I'm not changing my mind. I'm just..."

Devin dropped a light kiss on the tip of her nose. "Just what?"

She slowly shook her head, giving him a small smile. "Nothing."

Not fear, he decided. At least, not of him. His fiery and unpredictable lady wanted to be in control and was smart enough to realize that particular commodity went out the window when they were together.

"Good." Devin unbuttoned the strap of fabric at her neck and eased the zipper down. Kerry shivered as his fingers brushed a silky trail down her back. She hadn't worn a bra. He'd known it the minute he'd seen the dress, and the thought had driven him crazy all evening as she'd flitted from one group to another.

"Lift your hips, honey," he muttered against the thrumming pulse in her throat. He swept the dress down and tossed it on the floor. When she reached for him, he shook his head. "No. Don't move. Just let me look at you."

He took in her tumbled hair flowing over his pillow like sun-kissed brown silk, looking until her lashes fluttered and color stained her cheeks. Her lips were swollen and moist, soft as rose petals and tempting as sin. Naked except for a wisp of silky stuff that pretended to be panties, she was breathtaking, all feminine curves and hollows. Her pink-tipped breasts were small and full, her bottom sweet and lush.

He touched her with his fingertips, committing her to memory, skimming over the curve of her breasts, touching the tips until they hardened to ripe pebbles.

Helpless beneath his hands, Kerry closed her eyes. His fingers trailed down her rib cage and across her stomach, softly, as if she were a work of art and he a sculptor.

Devin felt the kick of her heart in his own when his hand moved lower, brushing away the scrap of fabric at her hips. As greedy as he was to watch the elegantly erotic way she shifted and turned, to see the expression of dazed wonder in her expressive eyes, he closed his own and stroked her.

When his fingers drifted lower and touched her soft, slick center, he felt the jolt again. Felt her taut anticipation, the unutterable tension. Felt the racing blood beneath her skin, the soft cry at the back of her throat. Felt not only her hands clutching him, but her astonishment, the dark delight, her flash of panic.

"Devin! Wait." Her voice was a breathless whisper, her hands slipped to his chest, pushing.

"What?" He groaned, and with a massive effort he stopped, moving his hand away, waiting.

Kerry scrambled to her knees in the middle of the bed, naked, breathless, tousled. The most beautiful thing he'd ever seen. She grabbed his hand and tugged until he joined her, knee-to-knee.

She went to work on the buttons of his shirt, her fingers impatient, shaking with need. A button popped off and she made an exasperated sound.

"Hey, what's the hurry?" Devin covered her hands with his and grinned when she shook them off. This was a first, he decided, hoping it wasn't the last. He had never had a woman so anxious to get at him that she tore off his clothes.

When Kerry pushed it off his shoulders, he obediently shrugged out of his shirt and tossed it aside. Then he wrapped his arms around her and pulled her close, groaning when the taut tips of her breasts prodded his chest. Kerry leaned into him, needing his heat, his touch.

"Hold me, Kerry. Put your arms around me and hold me."

"In a minute." She parted her lips for his kiss, sighing when his mouth covered hers. Her hands flattened on his chest and slid down over his lean, hard stomach, her fingers gliding through a cloud of crisp hair.

She hesitated a moment when she reached his belt buckle, then went to work. After a brief, silent struggle, the two ends parted.

Devin raised his head, as breathless as Kerry, just as she unhooked the waistband of his slacks. He sucked

in his breath at the movement of her fingers against his
flesh. Another first, he thought, capturing her hands
and holding them still. No woman had ever tested the
limits of his control the way this one was doing.

Glorying in her impatience, he asked, "Are we in a
hurry here?"

"Just evening the odds," she murmured, flicking
her hair away from her face with a quick toss of her
head. Just as swiftly, she pulled a hand clear and
reached for his zipper.

"Wait." He flinched when her fingers closed around
the tab. "Damn it, Kerry, *easy!*"

She leaned back, sitting on her feet, hands resting
on her knees. "Then do it yourself. A few minutes
ago, you had me ready to fly, and this is one trip I'm
not taking alone."

Seven

The lady would definitely not fly alone. Not this time.

Devin got rid of his clothes, skimming off his slacks and briefs with one motion. He kept his eyes on Kerry's face the entire time, saw her eyes widen and heard her indrawn breath.

"Devin?" Still on her knees, she held out her hand.

He didn't know if she'd had second thoughts or was impatient, but he took no chances. He linked his fingers with hers, sprawled beside her, and tumbled her down next to him. "I'm here."

"Me, too." She touched her lips to his shoulder.

Devin felt it again. Her jittery anticipation, the wash of need. The edgy nerves. He leaned over her, soothing with his hand and mouth, tracing the feminine curves until only the need was left.

Tenderness, he thought. If ever there was a time for it, it was now. He would go slow, go easy. Take his time and show her how romantic he could be.

That was the plan—and it only lasted until she touched him.

When Kerry trailed her fingers across his chest and followed the arrow of hair down his stomach to where it widened, the plan gave way to consuming need—his need this time. Passion, and the need to possess, took over. Possess her here, now, before he was torn into shreds of desperation.

He held her close.

She wrapped her arms around his neck and pulled him closer.

With her slim body molded to his, their legs tangled, he ran his fingers through her golden brown hair. His hands were unsteady while his mouth tasted, devoured her.

Kerry moaned, clinging to him, opening for him, shivering when his tongue met hers in an ancient and timeless duel. Hunger blossomed deep within her, sensitizing her to his slightest touch, even as she craved more. Her restless hands kneaded muscle, hard and resilient, beneath smooth skin and crisp hair. She gasped, trying to draw air into her aching lungs, willing to give up breathing, not wanting him to stop the incredible things he was doing. His touch was pure pleasure, a pleasure so deep it was close to pain.

She had never been wanted like this. Not this way, with such hunger, with such need. With such intent to give as much pleasure as was taken.

When his mouth found her breast again, he groaned, feeling her pleasure, the kick of hot excitement. She writhed beneath him, and he knew the plan was a lost cause. Slow and easy had no place in the scheme of things tonight. Not when Kerry had her legs wrapped around his hips and was chanting his name with every breath.

He slid into her and heard her sharply indrawn breath. "Kerry?" With muscles tensed, he poised above her, hauling air into his lungs. "Did I hurt you? Kerry? Damn it, say something."

She shook her head, frantic with need. "No. Devin... I... Don't... stop. Not now." She took a shuddering breath. "Not ever."

Devin agreed. "Never, babe. Never." He moved in a shattering rhythm, Kerry matching him stroke for frantic stroke.

Kerry's nails dug into Devin's shoulders as her body filled with incredible tension, and she followed the siren song in a dance that spiraled higher and higher, her body in perfect harmony with his.

Then she convulsed around him and the song was silenced by her wild cry, the dance ending on a frantic note. Devin buried his face in her throat and followed.

His lady hadn't flown alone. On any of the flights.

That was Devin's first thought the next morning before he even opened his eyes. Kerry was a warm, distinctly feminine bundle curled up against him, her head on his shoulder, her arm lax across his waist. She smelled of wildflowers and the musky scent of a well-loved woman.

He had learned more about her last night than she would ever suspect. More than he had expected. But it would have been difficult not to, with her emotions invading his head and playing havoc with his body.

Kerry had been astounded to discover that she was a highly sensual woman. And the fact that she had made the discovery in his arms was the main reason for his present state of masculine satisfaction, he admitted silently, running his hand down her thigh. She had been hot and wild, trembling in his arms one second, daring him, pushing him to the brink the next. And each time she had gone over the edge, he had been with her.

Whatever relationships she had experienced in the past, it was clear that last night had represented several firsts, he reflected as he gazed out the window, watching the lacy leaves of a jacaranda sway in time to the soft breeze. That knowledge was also a source of satisfaction. And pleasure.

At least it was until he examined it more closely.

Frowning, he admitted he didn't like the idea of Kerry with a man. Or men. Except him. Even if they had been thickheaded fools, incapable of bringing out her latent sensuality and depriving her of the wild excitement that went hand in hand with such a nature. Idiots, he decided, dismissing them with a shrug.

Thank God.

His frown deepened as the men refused to remain dismissed. Kerry was twenty-seven and had never married. How many partners had she had in that time? It shouldn't matter—but it did. He was in no position to pass judgment, he reminded himself, mentally reviewing his own past. Because, while he had been selective, he had not been celibate.

It wasn't a matter of condoning or condemning, he reasoned. It was a matter of accepting. And living with that acceptance. So, what it boiled down to was the famous bottom line.

Kerry was his.

Even a single man in her past was one more than he wanted to think about, but the operative word was past. The door to that part of her life was closed. Nothing that happened before counted. He'd only have a problem with it if someone opened the door and came looking for her.

Kerry yawned and opened her eyes, blinking when she saw his profile. Handsome but a bit grim, she decided. Especially after a night like last night.

"You're supposed to wake up with a smile on your face," she informed him drowsily. "It's off-putting for a woman to open her eyes and find the man beside her scowling. If she were the type to have an inferiority complex, it would be even worse."

Devin turned his head toward her, tightening his arm and hauling her closer. He grinned. "And do you have an inferiority complex?"

"I might have—before last night," she said with disarming honesty.

"And today?"

Her smile was slow and very feminine. "Today I know I'm incredible."

"You are, indeed, madam." He dropped a kiss on the tip of her nose and felt himself getting hard. "You are, indeed."

When he moved convulsively against her, she cast a knowing look downward. "I'm not the only one."

"We're a real pair, all right." He gave her another quick kiss and shook his head when he caught the expectant gleam in her eyes. "But I think we pushed your limits last night. It's been a while for you, hasn't it?"

Color sprang to her cheeks, and he grinned. Incredible she might be, but she was still easily embarrassed. He had a feeling it would get even worse in the next few seconds.

He was right. Kerry yelped and grabbed for the sheet when he sat up and threw it aside.

"What are you doing?" She looked around for something to wrap around her, finally settling for pulling a pillow in her lap.

Devin got to his feet and looked down at her, resting his hands on his hips. "Come on, let's hit the shower."

"For heaven's sake, Devin! Will you please put something on!"

"Why? I'd just have to take it off again."

Kerry kept her eyes glued on his face. She knew she looked hot and flustered. Well, damn it, she *was* hot and flustered. It was one thing to go crazy in the dark of night with a man you're crazy about, she told herself. It was another thing entirely to have him stand right in front of you buck naked. In broad daylight.

She sat clutching the pillow, blinking in dismay as her own words caught up with her. *A man you're crazy about?* She had to be crazy.

She was, she thought with a sinking feeling. She absolutely, positively was.

About him.

Groaning, Kerry buried her face in the pillow. Not now, she begged silently, aiming her grievance at a celestial troubleshooter—anyone who happened to be free. Not here. Not this one. After years of waiting for the perfect time and place, the ideal man, not a macho, domineering, take-charge private eye.

"Kerry? Honey? What's the matter?" Devin yanked the pillow from her grasp and tossed it aside. Tugging her up beside him, he studied her face, puzzled by the conflicting emotions swamping her. He settled for the most obvious.

"Embarrassed? Come on, let's take that shower. Then we can get into the clothes you're so concerned about."

"It's a darn good thing there aren't any men working here today," Kerry said, drizzling pancake batter into the hot skillet. She knew she was chattering. She had been since she'd walked into the kitchen and found Devin setting the small table. Had been since he'd stopped long enough to give her a long hug and a hard kiss.

It was the best way she knew to fill awkward silences. And since she had a feeling that any silence between them right now would be awkward, she kept talking.

"You had a towel on when you went upstairs to dress," he reminded her.

"Barely. I'm just glad I didn't run into a telephone man or exterminator. Both of them are due some time today." She put a plate of steaming pancakes on the table and sat across from Devin.

"I'm having some extra phone jacks put in," she said with determined brightness. "And I'm starting a monthly spraying program to keep the creepy crawlies under control."

"Kerry?"

"More syrup?"

"No. Kerry?"

"Coffee?"

Devin shook his head, but he took both the pot and her hand. He set the pot aside and tightened his grip on her fingers. He attributed the turmoil emanating from her to embarrassment.

"We have to talk," he said quietly.

She tugged at her hand and sighed when he refused to relinquish it. "You are a man for talking, aren't you?"

"Not always."

Kerry felt her face go hot. He was right. There had been little conversation during the night. Very little. They had both touched, stroked, asked and demanded with their hands and bodies. The stunning pleasure they'd shared had not been the result of words.

"Talk to me, Kerry."

His gaze was as steady as his voice. Both let her know that they'd stay at the table for as long as it took.

Kerry dropped her fork, wincing when it clattered on the plate. "Devin, I'm no good at this kind of thing. Too much has happened between us too soon. To be honest, I haven't had much practice at this. I don't know what to say."

"You can start with what happened between the time you went upstairs and came back down."

Lifting her cup, Kerry stared at the contents, knowing exactly what had happened. She'd had time to think. She'd had time to realize that falling in love was serious—especially when she'd only known the man for two weeks. She'd had time to get scared.

Since she wasn't crazy enough to share her thoughts, Kerry took refuge in her job. "I have work to do," she said bluntly.

Devin's brows rose. "I wasn't planning to chain you to a bed," he said in a mild voice.

"You already interfere. You upset my schedule. If you had this kind of hold over me, God only knows *what* you'd do."

"What kind of hold?" His voice was very soft, a trap waiting to be sprung.

"If we were . . . lovers."

"We *are* lovers, Kerry. And that's not going to change."

Her eyes narrowed. "Don't I have a vote in this?"

"Nope." Devin shook his head, ignoring her enraged gasp. "You voted last night. And you said yes."

"Well, I changed my mind."

"You can't. Oh, you can change the words, all right." His blue gaze held hers until she blinked. "But you can't change the way you feel."

Kerry tensed. "You have no idea how I feel." Thank God. That was a weapon she definitely wasn't handing over.

"Sweetheart, I was there in bed with you, remember?" Devin began to relax now that he was on solid ground. "I felt everything you felt last night."

"Well, it's nice to know we're on the same wavelength," Kerry grumbled.

Devin refilled their cups, then put the pot aside. He took her hand again, stroking the backs of her slim fingers with his thumb.

Timing, he thought, watching her face. It was everything. He had learned that a long time ago. There was a time to wait and a time to move. And right now, after last night, was the time to talk. She would listen. And understand.

"That's not what I meant," he said quietly. "I didn't just react the same way you did, I felt what you were experiencing. The anticipation, the hunger, the need. All of it. Everything."

"How nice," she said inadequately, color washing her cheeks again. "Then we both had a...good night, I take it."

"I'd say it fell more along the line of spectacular," he said equably, knowing she still didn't understand.

Kerry made a frustrated sound, but she didn't retreat. Gripping his hand, she said, "Devin, I'm making a mess of this. I told you I'm not used to these morning-after sessions, and, damn it, I just don't know what to say to you."

"Tell me how you felt last night. Don't think about it, just let loose with the first word that comes to mind."

"Wonderful." Her gaze met his, then skittered away. "That's a stupid word. It doesn't begin to express it. I felt like a priceless piece—"

"Of porcelain."

She nodded absently. "Like an—"

"Amazon."

"A primitive woman—"

"Claiming her man."

Kerry caught her breath and her startled gaze met his. When she tried to jerk away, Devin's fingers wrapped around her wrist, holding her.

"What are you doing?" she whispered.

He saw the uneasiness flicker in her hazel eyes and wondered if he had miscalculated. Well, if he had, it was just too damn bad. Another thing he had learned a long time ago was once you'd made your move, there was no going back.

"Just telling you I understand."

She shook her head, her uneasiness escalating to outright alarm. "You're doing more than that. You said words that I was still groping for. Devin, what the hell is going on here? How did you know what I was going to say?"

"Calm down, Kerry." He swore softly, keeping a firm grip on her wrist. "That's what I've been trying to tell you."

"Tell me what?" She groped wildly for an explanation. Grasping at straws, she said, "That you're a mind reader?"

"Not exactly." He winced when her eyes narrowed.

"Then what, exactly?"

Devin sighed in exasperation. This wasn't going the way he'd planned it. "More of an emotion reader," he finally said.

"I beg your pardon?"

Shock crossed her face. It was followed by disbelief—and a strong urge to escape. As always, he didn't have to see the emotions. He felt them a beat before they made it to her face.

"Emotions," he said levelly. "I feel them."

"From everyone?" Her hopeful tone made it clear that she didn't want to be singled out.

He shook his head. "Only Megan—"

"Because you're twins," she offered tentatively. "That makes sense. I guess. As much of any of this does."

"And now, you."

She jerked at her hand again, and had no more luck than she'd had before. "Devin, this may come as a surprise to you, but I don't want to be on your list. Just keep it in the family, okay? Scratch my name off. For that matter, scratch *me* off, and let's forget about the whole thing. Don't keep shaking your head. I'm serious!"

He kept his voice soothing, to calm the panic racing through her. "Sweetheart—"

"Don't call me sweetheart."

"That's not the way it works."

"You mean there's a system to this thing?"

"Sort of."

"Sort of," she mumbled, lifting her eyes upward in supplication. "Why me?" she asked morosely. "Why the hell *me?*"

Devin didn't feel very celestial, but he made the effort. "Just lucky, I guess."

"Sure." She rested her elbow on the table and propped her chin in her hand. She made no effort to disguise her wariness. "All right, tell me about this 'sort of' system. And while you're at it, fill me in on how I got caught up in it."

Devin shrugged. "As far as Meg and I are concerned, we were born with it. Grew up with it. If one of us got in trouble, the other one knew it. It was the same with any strong emotion. We rarely know the reasons, but we tune in to the feelings. So it's not a mental thing—we're not reading minds—we *feel* the actual emotions."

Kerry groaned. "I want to go on record here as being a skeptic. I don't believe this stuff really exists."

"I know." Devin grinned. He couldn't help it. She was so damn cute.

"But apparently you do."

He lifted his shoulders in a small shrug. "What can I say? I've got it."

"So, for the sake of this conversation—weird as it may be—let's pretend that it does exist." She waited for his nod. "How long did this thing last between you and Megan?"

"Forever. We still have it. At least, I think we do."

"Think?" she inquired delicately before taking a swallow of coffee.

"Yeah. I haven't picked up much from her lately. Everything I'm getting is coming from you."

Kerry's eyes grew big over the rim of the cup. When she choked, Devin took her cup and set it down, watching her with narrowed eyes.

"You okay?"

"Fine." Kerry wiped her watery eyes. "Just fine. I'd be even better if you'd tell me how *I* got involved."

Devin ran a hand through his hair. It was the only sign of agitation he allowed himself. Kerry, he decided, was wound up enough for both of them.

"Damned if I know. One night I woke up out of a sound sleep and there you were."

"Doing what?" She eyed him with deep suspicion.

"Being scared," he said succinctly. "It was your first night at Rainbow's End."

Kerry's expression was deeply, profoundly thoughtful. "You mean," she said finally, "that you've been—"

Devin held up his hand to stop her. "I don't know how else to say it. I've been picking up on your emotions, *feeling* them, since you got here."

"And that's why you've been popping up at the oddest times wanting to know if I'm all right?"

"Yep."

"And the telephone call the day my room was tossed?"

He nodded. "Same thing."

Sighing sharply, Kerry leaned back in her chair. "I don't believe in any of this," she reminded him.

He waited, watching the wheels turn.

"But I know you do."

"So—" her shrug was elaborately casual "—from your point of view, what do you think this means?"

He grinned. "That we're linked, baby. We're linked."

Kerry's expression grew even more leery. "Is that anything like being soulmates?"

Remembering her complaints about the man in California, Devin shook his head. "Nope. This is a real pain to me. I've got enough to worry about in this lifetime without chasing you through eternity."

Some of the tension drained away, but she still eyed him cautiously. "How long do you think it'll last?"

"I don't know. A week, a month, maybe longer."
On the other hand, Aunt Elly was still tied up with her
stuntman husband.

"So," she said slowly, "what you're telling me is
that you can crawl in my head and tiptoe around anytime you want. Right?"

"Wrong. I only know what you're feeling. The
stronger the emotion, the clearer I get it. Your mind is
a total mystery to me. Hell," he said with sudden disgust, "if I knew what you were thinking, we wouldn't
be having this talk. We wouldn't have to. No, if you're
looking for a mind reader, give Megan a call."

"Megan?" She looked at him in horror. "My God,
that's right. She's got it, too."

"I wish you'd quit talking about it as if it were a
communicable disease."

She didn't allow his tone of mild complaint to di-
vert her. "And Luke?"

He shook his head. "Pure as the driven snow."

"How did he, uh, react when he found out about
Megan?"

"Spooked the hell out of him," Devin said cheerfully, glossing over the fact that Megan was bound and
determined to communicate with her husband the
same way she did her brother.

Kerry sat quietly, gazing at her cup, absorbing the
latest bomb he'd dropped. Finally, she looked up. "Is
there anyone else in the family who has this...stuff?"

"Let's give it a name, sweetheart." He forked up a
bite of his neglected pancakes and chewed thoughtfully. "It's called psychic ability and it takes many
forms. And, yeah, there are...several people who have
it. My mother and Uncle Loe head the list."

"Good grief."

He nodded, willing to give her as much time as she needed. "Something to think about, isn't it?"

"I don't know what to think," she admitted slowly. "I've always thought people who talked about psychic phenomena were as weird as the ones who claim they've ridden in UFOs."

"You don't believe in them, either?" When she just stared at him, he grinned. "Tell you what, some night we'll climb a mountain and look for them. I have it on good authority that there are a lot of sightings around here."

"Forget it. I have my plate full of psychics at the moment." She waited while he filled their cups. "I don't want to hurt your feelings," she said, obviously feeling her way. "But I really need to think about this. I'm finding it a little hard to deal with."

He nodded. "I have some books, case studies, if you're interested. You're welcome to look through them." He lifted her hand and brushed his lips across her fingers. "Sweetheart, I know it's a lot to swallow."

"Devin?"

He stiffened. Misery and regret were coming at him in waves, and if he didn't think of something fast, he was going to find himself on the front stairs with his duffel bag and computer. Holding up his hand, he said, "Wait a minute, Kerry. I've thrown a lot at you, and I know you're upset. You have every right to be. But I'm asking you not to make any decisions about us right now. Give it a little time and get used to the idea."

"Devin, it's not only that." She put her hands to her mouth in an almost prayerful gesture. "Before I came downstairs, I knew I had to say this." Devin opened his mouth, and she shook her head. "No, let me finish while I can.

"Last night was the kind of night every woman prays she'll have at least once in her lifetime. I'm one of the fortunate ones," she said simply. "But it happened too fast." She gave him a troubled look. "I don't want you to get the wrong impression. I don't *do* things like this. I don't sleep around—"

"Hell," he said roughly. "I know that."

"Especially with someone I've only known a couple of weeks."

"Can we get to the bottom line here before I go out of my mind?"

She nodded. "All right. I need time, and I can't make any promises."

"If you think I'm going to leave you alone in this place, you're crazy." He folded his arms across his chest and seemed to take root.

"I'm not asking you to do that." She gave him a faint smile. "Actually, I've gotten used to having you around." Her smile faded. "But I suppose that isn't fair to you, to stay here when—"

"That's my problem, not yours. I'll survive." For a while. "So it's settled? I'm staying?" His steady gaze dared her to argue.

Kerry nodded slowly. "As long as you understand that I'm not going to bed with you again unless I know it's the right thing to do. For both of us."

Devin stood up and leaned across the table, bracing his hands next to hers. Lowering his head, he covered her mouth with his. When he moved back, they were both breathing hard.

"Not unless, sweetheart. Until."

Eight

―――――

"Are you at it again?"

Kerry stood in the doorway between the kitchen and dining room, a long-suffering look on her face. She had stopped with the sole intention of admiring the large koa wood table delivered earlier that day but found the gleaming surface covered with her vacation photos. They had been arranged in stacks that had nothing at all to do with their original sequence, and Devin was studying the pictures with methodical intensity. He had preempted the only chair brought by the delivery men, a solid piece of furniture with a carved back that fit the casual elegance of the room.

And the man.

Devin was undeniably solid. And while he moved with an economical grace that approached elegance, he was also like a bulldog, she thought. Once he got his teeth into something, he never let go. It wasn't a new notion, she reflected. She'd had an inkling the day he'd moved in, and the following days had done nothing to change her mind. The past ten days—since her request, and his reluctant agreement, to put their relationship on hold—had merely enhanced and reinforced the opinion.

"Most of them aren't very good, you know," she said, coming closer to peer over his shoulder. She examined the pictures with frowning concentration. "I certainly didn't expect anyone to go over them with a magnifying glass."

He had confiscated the photos the day she'd finally picked them up, barely giving her time to go through them. He'd been studying them ever since.

Kerry tried again. "Devin, those are snapshots, not the Dead Sea Scrolls. What you see is what you get. They don't have any hidden messages."

"I think at least one of them does. It's just up to us to figure out what it is," he said absently, setting aside one colorful stack of sunsets and horizons and reaching for the next. "It's pretty obvious that someone wants something you have."

"I don't think—"

"And as you've pointed out on more than one occasion, it's pushing coincidence a bit far to think we're dealing with two sets of burglars. So let's think back to the hotel break-in." Devin sifted through the fistful of photos as he talked. "Nothing was taken, and the only things not in the room were what you had with you—your straw bag and camera. We can more or less eliminate the purse."

"Why? I had my wallet and credit cards in it."

"If that's what they had been after—"

"He," Kerry grumbled. "Let's call him he. It's bad enough thinking there's one person skulking around out there. I draw the line at dealing with a gang."

"He would have held up someone on the street," Devin finished calmly. "People like that usually avoid run-ins with hotel security. So, you tell me. What does that leave?"

"The camera." Kerry sighed at the depressing logic and darkly considered the idea for several long moments. Brightening, she said, "Or, maybe not. If that's what he wanted, why didn't he just follow me and grab it?"

Devin shrugged. "Any number of reasons. Maybe he wasn't good enough to keep up with you. Or there were too many people around. Or maybe," he added grimly, "you were just lucky. Damned lucky."

"Or maybe we're letting our imaginations carry us away."

"Don't sound so hopeful." He reached for the hand resting on his shoulder and brought her around to his side, urging her closer until she was standing in the curve of his arm. "I found more footprints this morning. Out behind the last cottage. So our visitor isn't going away." He felt the shock jolt through her and waited, tightening his hold on her, keeping her next to him.

"He's back?" Kerry leaned against him, unconsciously seeking the comfort of his hard body.

"He never left."

Kerry gazed at him, waiting until he met her annoyed gaze. "You mean to say," she said slowly, "that he's been wandering around all this time and you conveniently forgot to tell me?"

Devin shook his head. "I didn't forget, and there's been nothing convenient about this mess since it began. I didn't tell you because you had enough on your mind. On top of that, I figured he wasn't breaking in here as long as I was hanging around, so there was no reason for you to get upset. Is there something wrong with that?"

"Yes. Plenty. First of all, I'm the manager here, remember? It's my job to know what's going on— good or bad. Second—" she poked at his shoulder with a slim finger "—I'm not so fragile that you have to keep me in a plastic bubble. And third, I should have been told, if for no other reason than my own protection. What if he had been hiding by one of the cottages and I ran right into him? Knowing he might be around, I can at least be prepared."

"You're right," Devin said, trying to sound remorseful, deciding it was the quickest way to get through this and on to the next point. "Hell, I thought I had all the angles covered, and here I overlooked the biggest one of all."

Kerry scowled, not buying his contrite act for a moment. "I doubt that. Knowing your macho mentality, you probably thought you'd keep me in your pocket all the time and I wouldn't have a chance to get in trouble."

She was right, of course. That's exactly what he had thought, and it still seemed like a damned good idea. Kerry had the survival instincts of a butterfly. Probably even less. He studied her belligerent expression, wondering what she thought she would do if she *did* run into their nocturnal visitor. Talk him to death? Or invite him in for coffee and lecture him on the perils of antisocial behavior?

Well, macho mentality or not, he was going to give her the protection she needed, whether or not she believed it was necessary. One glance at her narrowed eyes told him everything he needed to know. She still thought he was overreacting. Thought that a chat with the burglar would accomplish more than muscle-flexing. And if open warfare broke out, she'd hold him responsible.

Devin shrugged, his hand heavy on her hip. "What can I say? I'm bigger, stronger, harder and tougher than you. For some reason that makes me feel more qualified to handle trouble. Crazy, isn't it?"

"No, Devin," Kerry said quietly, responding to the edge in his voice. "It isn't." She put her hand on his wrist, sliding her fingers over the crisp reddish brown hair, unconsciously soothing. "It's just hard for me to deal with. I've never been in a position where I needed to be protected, and I'm having a hard time believing that it's necessary now." She squeezed his hand and sighed. "I know I'm acting like an ingrate."

"I'm not big on gratitude. I'll settle for your trust."

Kerry's eyes widened in shock. "I'd trust you with my life!"

"You already are. I'm talking about trusting my experience when I assess a situation."

"Oh. That."

"Yeah, that."

"Well, it's just that my belief in human nature hasn't taken the beating yours has," she explained. "I'll try harder. And if you're right, if someone really *is* hanging around," she added with a grin, "you're the one I elect to stand between me and him."

"Sounds fair to me." He aimed a light swat at her bottom. "How cooperative are you feeling?"

Kerry groaned. "What? You want me to help you look for footprints?"

"No. I find too damn many of them on my own. I want you to take some time and tell me about these pictures." Without waiting for her nod of agreement, he patted his thigh and said, "Sit."

She groaned again. As she moved closer, she cast a swift glance around the room, knowing what she would find. Or more correctly, wouldn't find. Chairs. All but one had been back-ordered, and Devin had it.

They had survived the past ten days, Kerry was convinced, because she usually managed to keep a respectable distance between them. It hadn't been easy. Every time Devin looked at her, it was with a controlled hunger that shook her to the core. She was as grateful for the control as she was distracted by the gleam of hunger.

"How many times have we done this?" she demanded with a sigh, perching tentatively on his hard thigh. She was uncomfortably aware of the ripple of muscle beneath her as he settled back in the chair.

"Obviously not enough. Either you neglected to tell me something, or I didn't pick up on its importance. Let's start again." He pointed to a stack. "With these."

"Okay." She riffled through them quickly to see how he had organized them. "These are my people pictures. Human nature at work. I don't know any of the subjects. I already told you I was putting my new camera through its paces, seeing what I could do with the zoom and other goodies. I just took whatever interested me... to see what I could do without making people uncomfortable.

"This old woman, for example." She slid the first photo on the table. "Look at her beautiful skin and the faint lines fanning out around her eyes. I hope I look that good when I get to be her age. And this one." A young woman in a bikini was placed next to the old woman. "I never looked this good," she said dryly. "Quit drooling. You'll ruin the glossy finish."

His hand slid down the curve of her hip to her thigh, kneading, lingering. "I'll save the drooling for the real thing," he promised.

"The thought boggles the mind."

Adding a third picture, a group of college-age men, she said, "These kids were having a wonderful time working on a boat. It seemed like such a golden moment, a celebration of health and physical beauty."

One by one, she worked through the photos, indicating the point of interest in each. "Look at these." Kerry placed three of them side by side. "The pictures are awful, but the scene itself was cute. This man was playing with his dog." She pointed to the first, which captured a blurred profile of a small, dark man with his arm outflung toward the camera. Around his wrist was a chunky gold chain.

"As I said, awful pictures. I was trying to get the exasperation on his face and ended up with a large hand. The next is the dog. A golden retriever with a goofy grin. And the third is both of them soaking wet, the man still chasing the dog."

She went through the pictures, one by one, ignoring the inner voice reminding her of tasks waiting to be done, answering Devin's questions as thoroughly as she could. Referring to the time line they'd drawn up the first time they'd studied the photos, she said, "Yes, this was on Thursday. I went to the Arizona

Memorial and the Polynesian Cultural Center that day."

"And these?"

She shrugged. "As you see. Birds and flowers. I can't tell you when any of them were taken. Look, the zoom lens came in handy there." She pointed to the delicate yellow stamens of a bright red flower. "I thought I'd pick up some books later and try to identify them. And these are trees. Same game plan—buy books and identify. When people stay in bed and breakfasts, they always ask about the plants."

She stared at the photos and said thoughtfully, "That gives me an idea. I think I'll ask Mr. Kimura for a landscaping plan."

"A cheat sheet?"

Kerry grinned. "Whatever works. I can always do an in-depth study later. When things slow down." She started to get up, then promptly sat back down, her heart starting to thud when she realized Devin's fingers had closed on the waistband of her shorts.

"What's the hurry?" His voice was deep and slow.

A warning bell clanged inside her head. If you started with that question, she thought, then added the way he was holding her and the sound of his voice, the total was nothing but trouble.

She had been expecting it, Kerry realized with a faint sense of shock. Not consciously, perhaps, but now that he'd begun, she knew Devin wasn't about to stop.

She had watched him follow a trail on his computer, calling up one file after another with unruffled calm. She had seen him sift through piles of paper, looking for a missing piece of evidence, and she had observed his methodical manner of dealing with her snapshots.

But despite the evidence to the contrary, she knew that Devin was not a patient man. He might approach his work on that level, but his personal life was a different story. The very fact that he'd held off this long surprised her.

Astonish might be a better word, she decided after a moment's thought. Yes, she reflected with satisfaction, it was precisely the word.

But the not-so-patient man had waited ten days before deciding to push a little, and that spoke volumes for his control. The same control that glimmered in his eyes—along with hunger.

The thought of him losing a measure of it made her nervous. As a result, her voice was a bit higher than usual when she repeated his question.

"What's the hurry? I have things to do, and thanks to our little detour with the pictures, I'm behind schedule." Wondering if it would be that easy, she gave a tentative wiggle. His grasp tightened before she moved an inch.

"It's been ten days, Kerry. Ten days without you in my arms. Without you in my bed. How much longer is it going to be?"

Well, Kerry thought, stalling for time, what he lacked in patience he more than made up for in plain, simple, unvarnished and unequivocal language. Now, if she only had an answer that was as succinct and effective, things would be just dandy. Unfortunately, she didn't.

"I don't know." When the expression in his blue eyes hardened, she gave a helpless shrug. "Damn it, Devin, this is harder on me than it is on you."

"Don't count on it," he muttered.

"I have *never* gone to bed with a man I've known only a couple of weeks. Anyone with the brain of a butterfly knows it's a crazy thing to do. No, it's worse than crazy. It's stupid . . . and dangerous."

A look of shock crossed Devin's face. "My God, is that what you're worried about?" He cupped her face with his hands, tilting her chin up until her eyes met his. "Honey, I'm as healthy as they come, and one hundred percent safe. I can give you a gold-plated guarantee on it."

Kerry held up a hand to stop him, knowing that her face was undoubtedly as pink as her shirt. "I believe you. What I can't believe is that I did it."

"You did it because you wanted me," he said complacently. "You still do, as far as that goes."

"What an idiotic thing to say," she said crossly, shooting him a look of testy dislike. "Of course I did." She refused to give him the satisfaction of hearing that he was twice right. That she still did. "And that's the problem."

"Wait a minute." The satisfied gleam in his eyes faded. "I want to make sure I have this straight. We made love because we wanted and needed each other, and that's bad?"

She blinked, pleased that he understood. And surprised, she admitted silently. "Yes."

"Well, hell." He scowled at her. "You're crazy, you know that? Completely and certifiably nuts. What exactly do you want?"

Good question, she brooded, her surprise dissipating. She wanted a lot. First and foremost, she wanted his statement—that they had made love—to be true. From his standpoint as well as hers. Her thinking hadn't progressed much beyond that point. All she knew for sure was she wasn't much on one-sided affairs.

When it came right down to it, she wasn't big on affairs, period. In fact, a rather surprising thought had occurred to her more than once in the past ten days while observing some of the numerous birds flocking around the place—that emotionally, she was more closely aligned to the homing pigeon than any of the migratory birds.

And she was ready to build a nest.

The thought that had followed on the heels of that one had not been encouraging. Bachelors did not include nest-building in their top priorities, and if she had learned anything at the Murphy family night, it was that Devin was regarded as one of the island's most eligible and permanent bachelors.

She was told by more than one person that he had never before brought a woman to the gatherings. The comments had not been made with intent to hurt, she recalled. On the contrary. They had been congratulatory, as if she had pulled off the coup of the year.

Her life would be infinitely more simple, Kerry reflected, if she had indeed done such a thing. But the truth was, she hadn't. She had simply gone to bed with a man who wanted and needed her. A man who wanted to repeat the event as soon and as often as possible.

Once, an affair might have worked, she thought, shifting restlessly on his thighs. It would have been highly erotic and mutually satisfying. Yes, it could have worked—if she hadn't spoiled the whole thing by falling in love.

Devin watched the fleeting expressions cross her face and couldn't read any of them. Hell, he thought in disgust, he'd never been good at it. He didn't have the foggiest idea what she was thinking behind those troubled eyes. And the feeling she was radiating was turmoil—which told him exactly nothing.

"Kerry," he repeated more gently, but with an urgency that surprised them both, "what do you want?"

Kerry raised her hand, letting her fingers brush across his lips. "More time." She sighed and dropped her hand. "Just more time."

This time when she moved, he released her. "Where are you going?"

"Out." Realizing the single word sounded more abrupt than she'd intended, Kerry lifted her shoulders in a small shrug, adding, "I'm going to look for Mr. Kimura."

"Ah." His smile was strained. "The cheat sheet?"

"Exactly."

It was good to be outside, Kerry decided as she headed toward the back of the property. Away from the undercurrents that came from knowing Devin was always within calling distance. For the first time, she wondered what it was like for Devin to be at the mercy of someone else's emotions. Well, she qualified, not exactly at the mercy. Nothing would put him in a position like that.

But it couldn't be easy. He would have to be well-centered, or well-grounded, or whatever the correct terminology was these days. Which probably accounted for his interest in the martial arts, she thought, the sudden realization startling her. In addition to the physical side, there was the self-discipline, the philosophy of inner peace, essential elements for those who walked that particular path.

It might be a bit dramatic to say that what he had learned over the years had saved his sanity, but it had undoubtedly helped to keep things in perspective. She kicked at a couple of leaves that had escaped Mr. Kimura and his minions, wondering how it would feel to deal with her own emotions as well another person's.

Awful. Unbearable. A nightmare.

She remembered Devin telling her he'd been awakened by her feelings the first night she'd spent at Rainbow's End. Being scared, he'd said. She closed her eyes briefly, recalling the night. It had been more than fright. It had been flat-out, heart-thumping terror.

She shuddered, imagining herself in Devin's place, asleep one minute and jerking awake to someone else's panic the next—not knowing who or where it came from. No, it was definitely not something she wanted to try—not even once.

From Devin, her mind turned to the rest of his family. A mother, an uncle, a sister and God only knew how many more who read minds and the future with appalling ease. It was something else she had no desire to deal with.

As she approached the first cottage, Kerry's mind turned to more cheerful thoughts. Opening the door, she stepped inside and took a quick look around. Slowly, almost in layers, the rooms in all the cottages were taking shape. The textured plaster on the walls had been painted and carpets laid. Beds had been delivered and set up. She was making daily forays into town, hitting antique stores and estate sales, looking for accessories that didn't scream of newness. It was her job to finish what Megan had created, a nineteenth-century house that was charming and comfortable in the twentieth.

Kerry stepped outside, closing the door behind her. Mr. Kimura, she reminded herself. She needed to find him before he took off for the day. Following the path that meandered around the cottages, she headed for the jungle-like area he had just begun to clear.

She took a long, deep breath and let it go, trying to shake off some of the tension that tightened her shoulder muscles. Stress, the modern-day plague, she thought philosophically, stopping to pick a few sprays of orangy-pink Plumeria for the house. No one escaped it. In her case, it wasn't caused by hard work or long hours. Those were conditions she thrived on. No, any stress she was dealing with these days was the result of her troublesome lover. Having him around the house twenty-four hours a day was getting on her nerves.

If it had been mildly annoying at the beginning, the pressure had escalated in quantum leaps these past ten days. There's nothing like a frustrated man to create gloom in a house and stress in a woman, Kerry reflected. She could feel the charged atmosphere as soon as she entered the house, and she didn't have an ounce of psychic energy in her body.

She was wondering what Megan would make of the tension, when two young men stepped out from behind a large hibiscus bush. Large, muscular and bronzed, they were wearing T-shirts, cutoffs and running shoes. One had on a red baseball cap, the other one wore blue.

Kerry smiled. "Hi. Have you seen Mr. Kimura?"

The two stopped on the path in front of her, glancing at each other. "Mr. Kimura?" red cap asked.

"Aren't you part of his crew?"

They shook their heads, and Kerry was momentarily distracted by matching pelts of thick, straight, dark hair.

"Don't I know you?" She tilted her head, studying their faces, frowning as a thread of memory nudged her. They were handsome and looked as if they spent their days hauling surfboards up and down the beach.

"Did I meet you at the Murphy's family party?" She gave an apologetic shrug. "I'm sorry, I don't remember your names."

"You never heard them," blue cap said.

"Oh. Well, I'm Kerry Cottrell, a friend of Devin's."

"Who's Devin?" This came from red cap.

Kerry's smile faded at the question, and a small chill worked its way up her back. Something was wrong. Very wrong. One of the things she had learned to deal with—sometimes with annoyance, others with gratitude—since she'd moved to the island was that everyone in the area either knew or was related to Devin. She had not met one person who'd needed an introduction.

"No," she said softly, "I think the right question is, who are *you?*" She took a step closer and blinked in surprise when they backed up.

When one of the young men stumbled on a lone tuft of grass in the center of the dusty path, Kerry glanced down.

"My God," she whispered, her eyes widening as she recognized the crisscross running shoe tread she'd last seen on her kitchen floor.

Nine

Omigod.

Sheer panic shot through Kerry as her fascinated gaze traveled from the incriminating prints to the two brawny men planted in the path before her.

Omigod.

Devin had been right. She *was* smaller, softer and slower than he was. And scared. What the hell was she doing out here alone with these two?

Before she came up with an answer, her memory kicked in, leaving her with an image of sunlight on the water, a brisk breeze and waves frothing on the sand.

"I know you," Kerry said impulsively. "You were on the beach that day, with a couple of other guys, working on a boat. I have a picture—" She broke off in dismay when the two men exchanged glances. Devin was going to kill her, she thought dismally. Strangle her with his bare hands.

If these two didn't beat him to it.

"That's why we're here," blue cap rumbled. "The picture," he clarified when she blinked up at him.

"Oh," Kerry said slowly, her mind racing through her options. Only one looked good. "Would you like to see it?" she asked politely.

Blue cap nodded. "Yeah. For starters."

"Okay, why don't you just...*catch!*" Kerry hurled the sprays of Plumeria at the men. When they instinctively raised their hands, she whirled and ran back down the path the way she had come.

"Hey, wait a minute!" one of them yelled.

Kerry broke into a smooth, long-limbed stride that was a remnant of her college track team and her one current form of exercise. As the sound of heavy feet thudding down the path behind her grew louder, she veered to the side and sped recklessly through the tangled growth.

"So where is Houdini when I need him?" she muttered breathlessly, racing toward the house. What was the use of having a psychic around the place if he wasn't around when she needed him most? The man had driven her nuts, popping up when she'd least expected him, appearing soundlessly in a room when she'd confronted a spider, and now that she could actually use him, he—

A large hand clamped around Kerry's arm when she sped by the thick trunk of an ancient tree, bringing her to a jolting stop. When she yelped, Devin covered her mouth with his other hand and pushed her to the ground.

"Be quiet," he said softly. "Not a sound."

Kerry landed on the grass on her hands and knees. Nodding, she stayed there until the adrenaline roaring through her body slowed down to a muted rumble. When she heard the two men pounding closer, she fleetingly thought of offering Devin her help. A second thought convinced her to remain where she was. She would only get in his way, she decided.

She was right. When she got to her feet and turned around, it was to find the two men flat on their backs, gasping for air, and Devin standing over them.

"Stay there," Devin told her, keeping his cool gaze on the groaning men. "Just in case they get any cute ideas."

"What did you do to them?" she whispered.

"Nothing fatal," he said carelessly. "They'll be fine as soon as they get some air in their lungs." He prodded one of them with his foot.

"Should I go call the police?" Kerry asked.

One of the men opened an alarmed eye and shook his head.

"Let's wait until they can talk," Devin said, his gaze thoughtful. "Until they answer some questions." At the sight of his cold smile, the alarmed man grew even more agitated. He gasped and made a strangled noise.

Figuring the men were not going to be a problem for a while, Kerry smiled at him. "You found me," she said in a pleased voice.

"I always do."

"What was it like this time? How did you know I needed you?"

"I heard you scream."

"I did no such thing," she snapped, taking an indignant step forward. Devin's heavy hand on her shoulder stopped her.

"That's what it felt like."

She thought about that for a long moment. "But how did you know where I was?"

Devin gave an absent shrug, watching the two men struggle to sit up. "I always know."

"That's spooky," Kerry told him. "Helpful in this case, but definitely spooky."

"And weird?" The corners of his mouth kicked up. She nodded. "That, too."

"You forgot bizarre."

"I was getting to it."

"Let's cover it later, okay? I think our friends have decided they're going to live."

"Uh, Devin?" Kerry swore silently, knowing he'd pick up on her jingling nerves.

"Yeah?"

"What are we going to do with them?"

"Take them back to the house and listen while they tell us a story."

"And then?" she asked, aware that the men were listening intently.

"We'll see," he said grimly. "All right, you two. On your feet." He hauled them up with an ease that had Kerry blinking, and prodded them forward.

Once in the house, everything seemed to change, Kerry observed thoughtfully. With Devin in charge, nothing seemed as frightening. The two men sitting side by side on the sofa, wincing occasionally, became Dwayne and Chris, college students.

"It's all my fault," Dwayne volunteered hoarsely as he rubbed his throat.

"We all agreed," Chris reminded him.

"Yeah, well, it was my idea."

"What was your idea?" Devin asked, settling back in his chair. It looked like it was going to be a long afternoon.

Dwayne leaned forward, absently rubbing his ribs. "Lightening up the boat." He turned to Kerry. "Our dads had signed up for a seniors' race and we thought—hell, we didn't think. We just decided to do it."

"Is that what this is all about?" Devin demanded, his narrowed eyes going from one to the other.

The boys nodded. "Yeah."

"Wait a minute." Kerry sat forward in her chair. "Let me get this straight. Your fathers were going to be in a boat race, one with a weight requirement for the boat, and you decided to—"

"Lighten it," Chris said. "So it would go faster."

Kerry blinked. "Isn't that illegal?"

The three men grinned. "Yeah, it is," Devin finally drawled. "But it happens a lot."

She frowned at them. Men, she thought disgustedly. Trust them to find something funny about the situation. Turning to the boys, she said, "I take it your fathers wouldn't have approved?"

Dwayne shook his head. "Actually, they're pretty good. They didn't need our help."

"Then why did you do it?"

Chris spoke up. "We'd all had a little too much beer and it just seemed like a good idea at the time."

"And right in the middle of things, I came along with my camera?"

"Yeah." Dwayne nodded. "That sobered us up pretty quick."

"I can imagine," she said dryly. Then, with genuine curiosity, she asked, "What on earth did you think

I was going to do with the picture? Blackmail you? I didn't even know what you were doing."

"Nah, it wasn't that. All of a sudden we realized how pi—" He cleared his throat and glanced apologetically at her. "How ticked our dads were going to be."

"And disappointed?" she asked gently.

Dwayne shifted uncomfortably on the sofa. "Yeah, that, too. Anyway, it wasn't worth it, so later we put the canoe back the way it was."

"How did you find out Kerry was here?" Devin asked.

Dwayne grimaced at the coolness of the older man's voice. "One of the guys followed her back to the hotel that day. He knew one of the bellhops and slipped him a few bucks to find out her name. We didn't know what we were going to do, but we figured we'd better keep an eye on her. When she left, he gave us her forwarding address. After that, we took an island hopper whenever we had the chance and came over." He shook his head in disgust. "Hell, it was stupid, I know, but we just wanted to get rid of the picture. We figured with it out of the way, the whole thing would be over."

"A guilty conscience really plays havoc with your nervous system, doesn't it?" Kerry smiled sympathetically, ready to forgive them. She knew from experience how an impulsive action could have haunting repercussions.

Devin wasn't so understanding. "Did it ever occur to you that your parents would like a charge of breaking and entering even less than messing with a boat?"

"We, uh, didn't exactly look at it like that."

"Terrific," Devin said. "How, exactly, did you look at it?"

Dwayne nervously adjusted his cap. "Well, we were doing more hiding and looking than breaking and entering. The only time we came into the house, it was open. Even the doors. Not that it did us any good. The place was empty." He looked regretfully at Kerry. "Except for your room. And I'm sorry we left it in such a mess. We were looking for the pictures when you drove up. It scared us and we just dumped everything and got out."

"What about the hotel room?" Devin said coolly. "You can't tell me that door was open."

Dwayne blinked. "What hotel room?"

"Where she was staying."

"You mean someone broke in there?" When Devin nodded, Dwayne flexed his fingers nervously on his thighs. "Not us," he said definitely. "Swear to God. No way. You think we're crazy enough to try something like that?"

Devin's voice was dry. "The thought crossed my mind."

Kerry brushed talk of the hotel room aside. "Once I got here, why didn't you just knock on the door and ask me for the blasted thing?" she asked in exasperation.

"We were going to." Dwayne shifted again.

Kerry sighed. "What stopped you?"

"We thought they might be in the car and—"

"You cracked the window."

"Yeah. After that, we figured you wouldn't be too happy with us."

"I probably would have strangled you. Or tried to." Kerry tilted her head thoughtfully, studying his apprehensive expression. "You sent the money for the repair work, didn't you?" she asked gently.

"Yeah. Was it enough?"

She nodded. "Plenty." Turning to Devin with a challenging look, she said, "Well, the way I see it, aside from scaring me half to death and causing us both a lot of inconvenience, they haven't actually done any harm. What are we going to do with them?"

"I'll think of something," he promised, grinning when the two boys paled.

"You do that. Make it good." She stood up, waving for them to remain seated. "Excuse me for a minute. I'll be right back." She walked out the door and headed for the dining room, listening to the rumble of Devin's voice, wondering what gruesome penance he was inflicting on them.

When Kerry returned, Dwayne and Chris were gazing at Devin. Their expressions made her think of prisoners whose executions had just been commuted. The three men rose with instinctive courtesy when she came into the room.

Handing Dwayne an envelope, she said, "Both the picture and negative are there. I suggest you get rid of them and forget the whole thing. That's what I'm going to do."

Several minutes later, she and Devin stood on the front porch, watching Dwayne and Chris trot down the road to where they'd hidden their car.

"I don't know about you," she said, "but all that youthful gratitude has worn me out." That, and a sense of relief.

"Uh-huh."

"What did you do to make them look at you as if you were the original white knight?"

He stared after them for a long, considering moment. "They got off easy and they know it. They're going to be Tony's unpaid labor for the blessing. Setting up and taking down four hundred folding chairs and a bunch of tables will keep them busy. They're also the cleanup committee."

"Brilliant. They'll work their tails off." Kerry smiled, thinking of the whoop of relief they'd let out as they started down the road. "They're not bad kids, you know. They just got caught up in something they didn't know how to handle. Maybe after they're done, we can give them a check."

Devin's brows rose. "Pay them? Not a chance. If they hadn't already come up with the money for your car window, I'd have taken it out of their hides. You were right about a guilty conscience eating at you, though. They need to make amends for what they did. Trust me on this."

"I do," she said softly, knowing it was the absolute truth. She trusted him with a readiness and a depth that should have surprised her, but it seemed the most natural thing in the world. She trusted him with her life. With everything—except her heart.

Kerry leaned against the porch rail, following his gaze down the road. She wondered what he was thinking. Something serious, no doubt. Serious enough to crease a frown between his brows, but his sphinxlike expression didn't give her a clue. His control was firmly back in place. Rather, she amended silently, it was *still* in place. No, she decided after another moment's thought, awesome as the idea was, his control was always in place.

"Hey." She nudged him with her elbow. "Lighten up. You solved the mystery. You were even right about the pictures. Gotham City is safe and the citizens can walk the streets again.''

"And you were right out in the middle of things. A walking target.'' He caught her in his arms and pulled her close, tightening his hold until she gave a muffled squeak of protest. "Damn it, Kerry, you could have been killed.''

Kerry braced her forearms against his chest and pushed. It was like trying to move a mountain. "Devin,'' she panted, "will you give me a little breathing space here?'' When his grip eased a fraction, she gave a huff and said, "They were just two kids. Two scared-out-of-their-wits kids. They wouldn't have hurt me.''

"Sure. That's why you were running, right?''

"I was running because I'm not a complete idiot. They were as big as trees, and I didn't know them from Adam. I wanted to get back to the house and let you deal with them. I told you if I got into trouble, you were elected to handle it.'' She deliberately kept her voice light, hoping to break the tension she could still feel in his hard body.

"Glad to know I'm good for something,'' he said with deceptive coolness. Without any warning, he wrapped his hands around her waist and tossed her over his shoulder.

"Devin! What are you doing?''

"Taking you inside where we can talk without being interrupted. Watch your head.''

Kerry clutched his belt with one hand and with the other caught the screen door before it hit her. "Put me down, you idiot. We're going to be interrupted by a couple of deliverymen any minute, and since you know everyone on this side of the island, it's going to be very embarrassing.''

"They've come and gone.''

"What?'' She thumped her fist on his back. "When?''

"While you were out playing games with college kids." Devin stalked through the living room, down the hall and into his room. Slamming the door behind him, he took a few more steps and tossed Kerry down on the large bed.

She landed with a bounce and came up swinging, her hands fisted. Before she could connect with his jaw, Devin had her flat on her back, holding her down with his weight. His large hand held her wrists together above her head.

"Let...me...*up*.''

Devin looked down at her furious face and almost smiled. But he couldn't. Not yet. She could have been hurt. He could have lost her. His heart hadn't found its way out of his stomach yet. His rational mind told him she hadn't been in danger, but he would never forget the sight of her running for her life with two men narrowing the distance between them with every step.

Kerry's head snapped around as she tried to settle her teeth in a vulnerable spot. Her hazel eyes were gold with fury, her hair sliding over his pillow with seething violence. "I'll get you for this," she raged. "I swear, I'll—''

"Hush," he soothed, brushing her hair back with fingers that shook. "Calm down, tiger. All I want to do is hold you. Kerry, I *need* to hold you.''

Slowly, as the intensity of his words reached her, Kerry stopped fighting. "You what?''

"I need to hold you. Just for a minute, okay?"

Adrenaline still zinged through her, making her gasp for air. Gradually, as her body slowed down, she began to feel more than Devin's confining weight. He was as tight as a drawn bow, fighting his own silent battle. Only this time, she realized, there was no visible enemy, no way to wage war and release the spring of tension gripping him.

As she softened beneath him, he released her wrists and slid his fingers through her hair, shaping her head, cradling it gently in his big hand. "You scared the hell out of me out there," he muttered.

She shuddered when he nipped at her earlobe. "I scared you? You were the one acting like Rambo."

He was hard, all muscle, without an ounce of softness. And part of him, she realized with a small sense of shock, was getting even harder. The shock immediately dissipated, replaced by a feeling of feminine wonder and delight. She was the reason he was in this state.

Not stress, not trauma.

He wanted her. Needed her. And his control was hanging by a thread.

She slid her arms around his neck, sighing when his mouth covered hers.

"Kerry?"

"Mmm?"

"You're driving me crazy."

"Good. That's just the way it should be." She looked up at him, her heart jumping at the promise glittering in his narrowed eyes.

"Kerry."

Her lashes fluttered at the seductive whisper and her lips curved in a small, very feminine smile. "Hmm?"

"Do you want me?"

Her eyes widened at the blunt words, and this time when her lashes lowered, it was to hide her apprehension. He was moving too fast. Again. She needed time to think. As usual.

Devin's lips brushed the hectic pulse in her throat. "Do you?"

Kerry nodded, closing her eyes to savor his touch. "Yes."

He muttered something that could have been an oath—or a prayer. "Now?" When his fingers moved to the buttons on her shirt, she leaned into his hand, wanting his touch on her bare skin.

"What?" Kerry blinked, trying to regroup her scattered senses. "Devin," she murmured hesitantly, twisting beneath his hands, "we need to talk. I don't think—"

"Good. Don't. We'll talk. I promise. All you want. Later."

Later would do, she decided hazily.

Later was good.

Later was fine.

Too caught up in her need to touch and be touched, she was hardly aware of her clothes being tugged off and tossed aside. Somehow Devin's were gone, too, and she was swamped by the heat of him, the hard muscles sliding under smooth skin.

Devin rested on his forearm and looked down at her, her parted lips, her closed eyes, the flush of color sweeping up from her breasts, and he tried to slow down. She deserved to be cherished. Every inch of her. Deserved to know how she touched something deep inside him. Deserved to have her uncertainties kissed away, stroked away, and he'd do it—even if it killed him.

It just might, he thought a moment later when her hand slid up his thigh, hesitated, lingered while her fingers drifted through the heavier thatch of hair. He shifted, moving her hand, dropping a kiss in her palm before he pressed it on the pillow beside her head.

Her lashes fluttered in protest, and his murmur was husky with promise. "Later."

His fingers skimmed the curve of her breasts, feeling her excitement when she shivered, saw it when the dusky tips of her breasts firmed and nudged his palm.

Kerry moaned, shifting restlessly when his hand drifted down, fingers lightly stroking a path between her breasts, down her belly to her knee. Her inner thigh, higher, higher. Touching, caressing, making her dizzy with pleasure.

She wanted to fly. To soar with Devin. To tumble down, taste the heat and fly again.

"Devin?"

"Hmm?"

"It's..."

"What?"

"Good," she gasped. "So good."

And it was. His clever hands moved over her until she shuddered with delight, then he soothed, calmed and started all over again.

And again. His mouth following the path made by his hands.

Until she could no longer bear the ache, the emptiness needing to be filled. Until her body moved in a slow, sinuous invitation he couldn't resist.

When he filled her, her breath caught and released on a sigh. They moved together, slowly, tenderly. The tenderness brought tears to her eyes that he kissed away.

Soon the tenderness became a spark, and a sultry rhythm that took them closer to the heat. And Kerry, clinging to him, tasted the fire and soared. She called his name, and he took her higher than she had ever dreamed of going.

Drifting awake, Kerry shifted lazily, reaching out. Devin was asleep, sprawled next to her, his lips pressed to her shoulder. He had his arm beneath her breasts, holding her close, as if even in sleep he didn't want her to get away. His heavy thigh lay across one of hers. She trailed her fingers down his back, smiling when his arm tightened, pulling her even closer.

She was lost. Sunk. Had gone down for the third time.

She was crazy.

She was in love.

With a man she'd known less than a month. She had never seen his condo, didn't know if he liked dogs, had never even had a date with him.

On the other hand, she'd slept in his bed twice, knew he was a good man in a crisis and . . .

He was a confirmed bachelor.

Yes, she was crazy, all right.

Devin shifted, kissing her shoulder. "Hi," he mumbled.

"Hi."

"You're soft. And sexy. And warm." He interspersed his words with kisses, working up to just behind her ear. "And I'm—"

"Hard." She shivered, thinking how easy it would be to lose herself in him and forget everything else. "Devin?"

"Mmm?"

"We have to talk."

Devin propped himself up on an elbow and looked down at her, his eyes suddenly alert. "Now?"

"Uh-huh. Now."

"I thought you told me earlier you needed more time."

"It ran out," she said simply, not even realizing she would say the words. But it was true. It was suddenly a matter of urgency to have things clear between them.

She pulled the sheet around her and sat up, drawing her knees to her chest and wrapping her arms loosely around her legs while Devin piled some pillows behind him and leaned against the headboard. He sat at an angle so he could see her face.

He caught the ends of her hair and, rolling them between his fingers, he said, "Okay. You first."

Kerry drew in a ragged breath. Her nerve endings jittered, and now that she had his attention, she didn't know where to start. "This thing we have between us," she began awkwardly. "You and me, we're—"

"Lovers," he said flatly.

"Lovers." She repeated the word softly, tasting it, testing it. Nodding, she said, "I suppose we are."

"Damned straight."

"And we're having an affair."

"You have a problem with that?"

She eyed him pensively. "It seems I do. It's a word I'm not really crazy about. It means no commitments, no promises, no guarantees. And no future."

"The hell it does."

"Think about it," she said quietly.

Wondering how things had gotten out of hand so quickly, Devin reached for her. He needed to hold her, touch her, believe that whatever had gone wrong could be fixed. Kerry stiffened and shook her head. Soon, he promised himself. He'd have her in his arms soon.

"Sweetheart, just tell me what you want," he sighed, dropping his hand.

"Marriage," she said baldly. "And a home, and a family. Oh, not necessarily with you," she added, lying through her teeth. "And not necessarily right away, but that's my goal."

Kerry eased her feet over the side of the bed and spotted Devin's shirt on the floor. Reaching down, she picked it up and quickly slid into it.

"Everyone who has seen us together has made a point of telling me you're a confirmed bachelor," she said, fumbling with the buttons. "Well, I guess that's fine for you, if that's what you want. It's not so fine for me."

"Kerry—"

She smoothed the shirt down her thighs and turned to him. "Be honest, Devin. Have you ever considered marriage when you've thought of me? Of us?" She gazed at his expressionless face. "I thought not," she said softly, walking toward the door.

Stomach churning, she turned back to him. "If you want an affair, you'll have to find another woman. And someday, when the time is right, if I'm lucky, I'll find another man."

It wasn't a bluff, she realized with stunning certainty. She wouldn't live half a life for anyone. Not even Devin.

Standing in the doorway, she said, "You see, I've learned something about myself in these last couple of weeks. I'm a permanent kind of woman, and I want something that will last forever. In the long run, I'd be no good at all at a hole-and-corner affair."

She took one last look at Devin, then turned and walked away.

Ten

"**K**erry? Where are you? We've got some talking to do, lady!"

Devin strode into the kitchen, surly and ready for battle. Damned if she'd get away with saying her piece then hightailing it up to her room for the night.

She wasn't there.

Morning sunlight streamed through the windows, coffee sat in the glass pot and a plastic-covered plate filled with muffins sat on the table. But instead of Kerry sitting in her chair, there was a note on the table.

He filled a mug with coffee, read the note and stalked back to his room. In seconds he was hunched over his computer, his fingers flying on the keyboard. Later, he stopped long enough to swear, take a long swallow of strong coffee and brood over the events of last night.

After Kerry had dropped her bombshells, he hadn't trusted himself to go after her. And although he'd wanted to rip off the door and haul her downstairs, he hadn't. Instead he'd done the safest thing for both of them—left her alone and worked through the night.

And now all he had for his efforts was a note telling him she was walking on the beach. If he hadn't already known, that would have been proof she was still upset. She hadn't once walked away from the job since she'd arrived. Hadn't taken a minute for herself.

He knew the path she'd taken—a back section of the property that had been neglected for twenty years or more. It meandered for roughly a quarter of a mile, dropped down the hill and crossed the old dirt road to the sand. Since Mr. Kimura's team hadn't reached it yet, it looked like a jungle. It would have been a simple matter to follow her, but he needed time as much as she did. It was probably a good thing she *had* gone.

If he saw her right now, he'd probably throttle her.

A hole-and-corner affair.

Damn it! There was nothing hole-and-corner about their affair. It wasn't some sleazy, two-bit, one-night-stand fling. Hadn't he steered her around the Murphy compound, showing her off to his entire family? And as for the rest of the accusations she'd flung at him, she was wrong. Dead wrong.

No commitments, no promises, no guarantees. And no future.

He was committed, all right. To getting her back in his arms. In his bed. And his life. As for the rest, he promised himself that he could guarantee she'd like it as much as he did. Want it as much as he did. The way she had yesterday. And eleven days ago.

And the future? She could be right about that one, he thought, leaning back in the chair. Without a rash, impulsive, exasperating woman in his life—without Kerry—there *was* no future. At least, not one that he wanted to consider.

Devin turned to the fax machine, scanning the material that had arrived the day before. The majority of it, sent by friends in the various island law-enforcement agencies, pertained to the dognappers.

He thought of what he had told Luke, that he was working on the matter. He was doing more than that, Devin admitted silently. He was pouring all of his frustrated energy into the search. It was better—and more productive—than wrapping his fingers around Kerry's slim neck.

Besides, it went against the grain to have one of his clients bilked. Even Mrs. Conroy, who had handed over her money without a whimper.

Devin's dark brows rose in silent speculation when he read the list of missing dogs attributed to the gang. They had been busy. The activity had started, he noted absently, several months before Kerry had arrived on the island, but had been on a decline the past few weeks. By the way the coordinated documentation was mounting, he reflected, it wouldn't be long before they were caught.

Maybe he was working on the wrong angle, he thought, flipping to the next page. Maybe he should have turned the investigation over to Kerry. The way she tore into things, she'd have them locked up and convicted within a week.

Kerry slowed down to a walk on the wet sand, breathing fast but not really winded. If she had run too far, she decided, it was all Devin's fault. After pacing her room for half the night, remaining there because she hadn't wanted another confrontation with him, she had needed to get out and run.

To make some decisions.

To figure out if she had well and truly screwed things up last night.

Devin was not the kind of man to receive an ultimatum well. On the other hand, she hadn't exactly delivered one. She had merely told him how she felt— what she could live with and what she couldn't. What he did with the information was entirely up to him.

There were times, she reflected moodily, when the male mind was totally incomprehensible. Had he actually decided at some point that he never wanted to marry, or had he just never thought about it?

Well, she had news for him. If he wanted her to stick around, he'd better start thinking. She was not about to take him to her parents and introduce him as her permanent live-in lover. Her family head count might run far short of his, but her parents had raised her to believe in old-fashioned values—love, marriage and children.

In that order.

She had gotten sidetracked, admittedly. It was hard not to, with a man like Devin. But when it was a time for tough decisions, the old principles kicked in.

And if he didn't think about it?

She lifted her shoulders in a small shrug, even though her heart clenched at the thought. If that was the case, then she had lost a gamble she hadn't even realized she was taking. But sometimes risks were necessary, she reminded herself stoically. And the results—good or bad—had to be lived with.

Somewhere along the way, early in life, she had learned that tact and compromise nicely smoothed out life's little bumps. But, later, she had discovered that tact didn't always cut the mustard and you couldn't compromise on principles.

Kerry came to a stop, looking back in the direction of the house. She couldn't avoid him forever, she thought with a fatalistic shrug. And she had a full day's work ahead of her. Be cool, she told herself as she trudged across the strip of sand to the road. Cool and friendly. Forget about last night.

Oh, sure, a small inner voice drawled sarcastically. *Forget that he makes you burn just by looking at you. Forget the way his body fits yours, turning you into a wild woman. Forget that with just his hand, just his finger, for heaven's sake, he starts a fire in you—and he's the only one who can put it out.*

Kerry wasn't noticeably soothed by the time she reached the winding dirt road. It didn't make her feel any better to see a large gray van speeding toward her. The road was on private property, and had once been used primarily for maintenance vehicles. Now Mr. Kimura's trucks paraded back and forth on it, and it would soon be a convenience for delivery men. Devin would not be pleased to see it being used for a speedway. Devin would not be pleased to see anyone on it who had not been security-checked back to their preschool days.

When the van slid to a halt just beyond her, Kerry put a friendly smile on her face and stepped forward to deliver a polite explanation regarding private property.

You're a confirmed bachelor.
The hell he was.

He had simply decided a long time ago that marriage probably wasn't going to work for him. He hadn't needed a wall to fall on him to get the point.

It had just taken three women to convince him— women he'd dated through the years and to whom he had eventually felt obligated to make certain explanations. Women who had been spooked by his link with Megan, spooked by the family "gifts," and had made no bones about telling him so.

After the third time, he'd made his decision. He appreciated women too much to become a hermit—or a celibate—so he would date and enjoy what he could for as long as he could. Then, before things reached an awkward stage, he'd leave.

And the plan had been a good one. It had worked. At least, it had worked until he'd met Kerry. He'd taken one look at her and forgotten his plan, his good intentions and whatever sense he had.

And now she was giving him hell because he wasn't married. Didn't the crazy woman realize that if he was, they'd be in a real mess? Whatever she thought about him right now, he had scruples. He wouldn't abandon a wife for another woman.

Not even for Kerry.

Kerry, the woman made for him as surely as flowers were made to bloom. Kerry, the one who melted at his touch. The woman who'd feared a man wanting a soulmate, only to find herself linked with a psychic. Kerry, the one who shot from the hip when she had something on her mind. The one who wasn't running from him.

"Well, damn," Devin muttered, surprised into dropping the papers he held. Of all the reasons she'd given before sailing out of the room, not one of them had had to do with his psychic ability.

He thought about that, filing it away, a hunter's gleam in his blue eyes, while he retrieved the scattered documents. He went through them again, systematically, acknowledging that something he had read earlier was nagging at him. Somewhere, on one of the papers was an item that had triggered a memory, a thought. It was important—or it would be when linked with another bit of information.

It was like a puzzle. A piece here, joined to a piece there, a little patience, and eventually the picture came clear. Devin turned to the next page, absently reaching for his mug. He was good at puzzles, always had been. He had the tenacity and the kind of mind that slipped information into slots, turning chaos into order. It was a useful talent.

He might even find it handy when dealing with a troublesome woman. Especially a troublesome woman who loved him.

Devin slowly placed the mug on the table, staring at it as if it had just turned into a crystal ball. Loved him? *Loved* him? His frown slowly lightened to a grin—a very masculine, satisfied grin.

Yeah. She sure as hell did. If he'd been able to think with his head instead of his hormones, he'd have known it a lot sooner. For a very simple reason. Kerry wasn't the kind of woman who could go to bed with a man, give herself so completely, if she didn't love the man.

Love *him*.

It looked like they had more to talk about than he'd thought, he decided, forcing his attention back on the papers spread around him.

Much later, Devin leaned back in his chair, silently gazing from the time frame he had drafted of Kerry's vacation to one of the reports.

It fit.

He checked the dates again and knew he had it. It was the answer, all right. It explained the hotel break-in, the gouged dining room windows and the different prints he'd found around the property. Dwayne and Chris had insisted they were not involved in those attempts, and he believed them.

The day Kerry had walked on the beach, taking pictures of the college terrorists and a man chasing a golden retriever, the police had received a call reporting the theft of an expensive dog. A young golden retriever.

Devin's gaze hardened. Yeah, it fit, all right, and it meant that Kerry was still being stalked—only this time by people more dangerous than a couple of scared college kids.

Kerry's smile slipped when two men climbed out of the van. One was small and dark, the other was a hulk with brown hair.

A sense of déjà vu swept over her as they walked toward her. It was not a nice feeling, she decided, recalling all too clearly the fear that had swept over her when Dwayne and Chris had seemed so threatening.

But they hadn't been, she reminded herself bracingly. And these men were probably just tourists who had turned off on the wrong road. They would be pleasant and grateful when she directed them back to the main boulevard.

She cast a quick look at the path leading to the house, noting with dismay it was well beyond the van.

If they *weren't* pleasant and grateful, and for some reason she had to make a run for it, she would have to pass both of the men.

Kerry took a deep breath as the men moved nearer. Obviously some of Devin's suspicious nature was rubbing off on her, she thought disgustedly. There was absolutely nothing wrong here. Just because she was alone with two unfamiliar men on a deserted road, with no one except Devin around for miles, it was no reason to panic.

Even if they were rather scruffy and—she took another look at the hulk—large. The smaller one was the neater of the two, she decided after another quick glance. He had on jeans, a long-sleeved knit shirt and running shoes. The hulk looked as if he had slept in the van for a week. His khaki shirt and pants were rumpled and stained, his green deck shoes were in no better condition.

"Hi," Kerry said brightly when they drew to a halt ten feet away. "Are you lost?"

"Not anymore," the hulk said. "Huh, Rollie?"

Rollie threw him a look of disgust. "Morning, miss. Nice day."

"A lovely day," she agreed with enthusiasm, trying to make up for her growing uneasiness. She gave them a quick smile. "But then, all of them here seem to be."

"Well," Rollie said, checking the blue sky approvingly, "you know what they say about paradise."

"No." The hulk shook his head. "What?"

"Never mind, Sam. Just forget it."

"Gee, Rollie, I just wanted—"

"I said, forget it."

"Okay, okay. All I wanted was—"

"Sam." The single word was quiet and menacing.

Kerry listened to the exchange with growing apprehension, frantically hoping that Devin, somewhere, somehow, was tuning in to it. Of course, he had made the distinction that he read emotions, not minds, but if her pounding heart was any indication, she was a shoo-in for a rescue attempt. And surely he wouldn't let a little argument stand in the way.

With determined cheerfulness, she said, "I know you gentlemen aren't aware of it, but this is a private road." Strolling to the center of the road, she gestured casually back in the direction they had come. "That's the way to the main street."

Rollie followed, still a few feet away, but between her and the van—and the path to the house. The hulk watched them.

Kerry didn't wait. She didn't know what they wanted, but she definitely wasn't hanging around to find out. Putting as much speed into it as she could, she took off at an angle, praying that Rollie wasn't as quick as he was small.

He was.

He grabbed her arm and tried to shove her to the ground, but Kerry fought, clutching his shirtsleeve and hanging on.

"Sam," Rollie panted as he wrestled with her, "get your butt over here and help me."

When Rollie's sleeve rode up and his chunky gold bracelet scraped her arm, Kerry blinked and promptly made the connection. This time she didn't mention that she had pictures of him—she had a feeling he already knew. She didn't know why they were important, but that was another thing she wasn't going to ask.

Terror washed through Kerry, and in its wake, adrenaline. While she was silently screaming for Devin, some part of her mind reminded her that she had three, four seconds at the most before the hulk shambled over. Once he got his hands on her, she wouldn't have a chance.

She fought like a wildcat, stabbing her elbow in Rollie's midriff. When he gasped, she stamped on his foot, grinding all her weight on it. He yelped and loosened his grip, and Kerry took off.

She flew down the road, fairly certain she could keep ahead of Rollie. Sam, she decided, was no threat at all. Not now.

Her confidence was abruptly shaken when Rollie let out a yell.

"Don't shoot her, you idiot. We need the pictures."

Guns. Good God, they had *guns*. Kerry veered off on the curving path, sending a panicky message to Devin as she scrambled up the hill. *When you come— and you damn well better make it fast—bring a gun. Maybe two.*

It never occurred to her to worry about Devin running into armed thugs. Devin was invincible. He was a one-man army. And he was taking his own sweet time coming to the rescue.

Devin swore, batting his way through the foliage. He really *would* wring her neck this time. What the hell was she doing out here, anyway? Whatever was happening, it wasn't fun and games. She was in trouble—big trouble, by the feel of it.

He met her at the crest of the hill, catching her when she tumbled over the top. He didn't give her time to slow down.

"Come on, this way." He hustled her down a narrower, less-traveled path, shoving ferns and large green fronds out of the way. "Who's after you?"

Kerry clutched his hand and followed. "The guy in the bad picture... with the dog and the gold bracelet. I don't know why."

"I do," he said grimly. "How many are there?"

"Two." She panted, matching his pace. He wasn't even breathing hard, she noted resentfully. "One's big enough to be three. And they have guns."

Devin shrugged. "You know what they say. The bigger they are—"

"Yeah, sure. Were they talking about giants with guns when they said that? And what the heck took you so long?"

"That's my girl," he said, flashing her a grin. "I come to the rescue, and do I get gratitude? Hell, no, I get a lot of lip for my pains."

He was enjoying this, Kerry thought incredulously, glaring at his back. The macho, rednecked idiot was *enjoying* it.

Devin came to an abrupt stop, and Kerry ran right into him. It was like hitting a rock wall.

"Now what?" she muttered, backing up a step and rubbing her nose.

"I found a place for you to roost while I go after those two." He pulled back a curtain of massive leaves and motioned her ahead of him. Kerry peered inside and saw a broad tree stump. When the leaves sprang back, it would be virtually invisible.

"Get in."

All of a sudden she wasn't sure she wanted to be left alone. "Devin, I—"

"In, Kerry. Now."

She got in and climbed on the stump, folding her legs and sitting Indian-style.

"Have you ever used a gun?"

She was shocked. "No! Never."

"Well, here's your chance. Here." He put a gun in her hands and folded her fingers around it. "Release this and pull the trigger if either one of them sticks his head in here."

She eyed it doubtfully. "What are you going to use?"

From out of nowhere, a wicked-looking knife appeared in his hand. "This."

"Oh, my God." One look at his face convinced her it would do no good to argue. "How are you going to find them?" she asked, batting at a huge leaf. "This stuff is awful thick."

Devin gave her a pained look. "Those two sound like bull elephants out there. How could I miss them?"

For the first time since he had caught her in his arms, she became aware of the two men blundering through the heavy foliage. They were nearer than she had thought.

"Rollie!" Sam bellowed. "Where the hell are you? I can't see a thing."

"Keep your voice down. I'm beside you, just a few feet away. Now shut up and find the girl."

Kerry watched Devin's face grow hard and knew that now wasn't the time to tell him she didn't think she could pull the trigger.

He dropped his hand on hers and squeezed. "I meant what I said," he whispered. "If they come, use it."

She met his gaze and nodded.

Devin lowered his head and covered her mouth with his in a hard kiss. "I love you, Kerry."

When she blinked at him, he stepped back and disappeared.

Kerry stared with growing wrath at the wall of trembling leaves. He *loved* her? And he couldn't find a better time to tell her? He couldn't tell her when he had her in his bed, shaking with need? He had to wait until he went off to war with a knife clenched between his teeth?

She was going to murder him, she decided, fury mingling with delight. And afterward, she would get a female lawyer and jury and tell the entire story. Not only would they not convict her, they'd give her a medal.

Minutes later, she was still staring at the leaves, plotting revenge, when the sound of labored breathing filled the air.

"Damned broad," Rollie muttered, swatting at the greenery. "How the hell am I supposed to find her in this mess of lettuce?"

Kerry stiffened, barely breathing. Her eyes widened in horror when her foot slipped off the edge of the stump, sending a crumbling piece of bark sliding across the damp soil.

Silently, staring before her, she brought her foot back up, not daring to breathe. Within moments, grimy fingers inched through the bank of leaves and slowly parted them. With a blaze of triumph in his dark eyes, Rollie stepped inside.

* * *

More through habit than necessity, Devin eased soundlessly through the damp foliage. Listening to the din ahead of him, he shook his head. He could be tearing through the place like a rampaging water buffalo and they'd never hear him.

Hoping grimly that Kerry would follow his orders, he veered to the left, tracking the bigger of the two men. She damn well better follow orders, he reflected, or that would be one more thing they'd be talking about. There was a time and a place to be hardheaded and independent. This wasn't it.

For the first time when tracking someone, Devin was distracted. Why had she looked so stunned? Didn't she know he loved her? Apparently not. Another item on the growing list of things to discuss.

He stepped over a small stream and gazed down at a print in the wet soil. It looked to be the size of a snowshoe. His brows rose in speculation. This time, Kerry hadn't been exaggerating—the guy was big.

It was not a print he had seen around the house. Probably his partner had been smart enough to know this one was as likely to fall through a window as open it.

Devin flexed his shoulders in an attempt to shake off the growing tension. Kerry's tension. He wished she'd settle down. He wondered how anyone lived with their emotions in such an uproar. One minute she was furious, then just nervous, then scared to death. It was enough to make a man jumpy.

A muffled oath drifted back to him and the thrashing stopped. Devin paused, waiting to see if the two men were joining forces. But there was just a loud, sucking sound, as if a large foot had been pulled out of the mud; then the big man grunted and started moving again, muttering curses with every step.

"Don't know why I get all the dirty work around here. What the hell is he doing while I find the girl, sitting on a lily pad?"

Devin followed, edging closer, listening to the rambling monologue.

"Feed the dogs. Clean up after 'em. Catch the damn things if they get loose. Sam, do this. Do that." His voice faded in another series of colorful curses.

Rollie, Devin thought, moving as silently as a ghost, you've got a real disgruntled employee on your hands here. As one boss to another, I can tell you, delegating the dirty work isn't always the smart thing to do. It can be bad for morale.

When Sam stumbled into a clearing, Devin followed him. He deliberately kicked a pile of leaves to get the big man's attention.

Sam spun around, his round face slack with surprise. "Who the hell are you?"

"Not someone you want to tangle with. Why don't you drop your gun and we'll go back to the house and call the police?"

Early as it was, Sam had had a bad day. He not only ignored Devin's advice, he spread his arms wide and, looking as big as a locomotive, let out a roar and charged him.

Devin waited until the last moment, then stuck out his foot and let the big man's weight take him headfirst into a tree trunk.

When Sam open his dazed eyes, he was tied hand and foot. Devin was on his haunches next to him, the tip of his knife pressed against his fleshy throat.

Devin gave him a cold smile. "You should have listened, Sam. I'm not in a real good mood. Whenever someone comes after my lady, I get upset. Understand?"

Sam's eyes bugged when the knife knicked him. He nodded violently.

"Good. I'm leaving you here for a while, and I don't want to hear a peep out of you. If I do, I'll come back, and I won't be happy. Got that?"

Sam nodded again, with even more enthusiasm. "Not a peep," he gasped.

It took Devin only a few minutes to cover the area and discover that Rollie was nowhere in sight. And it was too quiet. There was no way in hell that the man could be groping his way through the dense foliage without being heard. On his way back to the place he'd stashed Kerry, Devin considered the idea that Rollie had abandoned his partner and run. That was one possibility.

Deciding there was no sense in startling Kerry, he circled around and approached her hidey-hole from the back, silently moving the moist leaves aside and stepping into the small enclosure.

Devin blinked. There was another possibility that he hadn't considered, he realized. That his Amazon had captured her stalker.

He knew if he lived to be a hundred he would never forget the sight of Kerry sitting cross-legged on a stump with Rollie kneeling before her, his eyes crossed as he studied the muzzle of the gun pressed to his nose.

Devin moved behind her, reaching out to remove the gun from her white-knuckled fingers. "I knew you'd know what to do with this thing," he said laconically.

Kerry collapsed back against him with a sigh. "Well, it's like I told Rollie. I haven't had much experience with a gun, and I couldn't promise him a nice, neat hole in the shoulder. If he made me nervous, I knew I'd make a real mess of it."

After the police left with the two men and promises from Devin and Kerry to come in the next day and sign statements, Devin said, "Now, we talk."

They were on the front porch, and Kerry gave him a long look before she nodded and sat on the top stair. "Life is strange, isn't it?" she said thoughtfully. "My innocent day on the beach taking pictures caused all of this. I think from now on I'll stick to photographing trees and flowers."

"Sounds like a good idea. Those guys weren't going to give up. They couldn't give up. You had the one piece of evidence that could send them straight to jail."

"Definitely trees and flowers," Kerry decided.

"I'm not a confirmed bachelor," Devin stated in no uncertain terms.

"Could have fooled me." Well, wasn't it just like him to jump right in the middle? she thought disgustedly, scooting over to make room for him beside her. No leading up to a delicate subject, no softening the blow, just diving in headfirst. "That's what your family thinks."

"That's their problem. I've had my own." Resting his forearms on his knees, Devin gazed out over the yard and told her about his decision. "So, it's not that I have anything against marriage," he ended. "I just never thought I'd find a woman who could deal with this. And then I met you."

"You must have a rotten karma, Murphy," she joked feebly, astonished at the outrage pouring through her. She'd like to yank those women bald-headed. "You met me at a bad time. I was running from a metaphysical bookstore owner, complete with psychic sidekick, who nagged me about being his soulmate. I was not a happy camper."

He nodded complacently. "Bad time or not, I was right. You're not afraid of it, are you?"

"Of your psychic ability?" She gazed at him, smiling thoughtfully. "It's come in pretty handy lately." Sobering, she said quietly, "No, I'm not afraid. I've read a few of the books you gave me, and while I'm surprised at some of the stuff—"

"That's natural."

"And skeptical about others—"

"That's healthy."

"I'm not afraid."

"Good." He reached for her hand and dropped a light kiss on each of her fingertips. "Now tell me why you got so mad when I told you I loved you." He felt her trill of nerves and kept her hand firmly in his.

"It was where you told me," she finally said. "Why couldn't you have told me when we were making love?"

Devin looked astounded. "I thought I had."

Kerry rolled her eyes and muttered, "Men." Narrowing her eyes, she said astringently, "What you told me is that you needed me, wanted me."

He waited for the punch line. When none came, he said, "It's the same thing."

"Maybe to a man. What a woman hears is he wants her body and doesn't much care about the rest."

"For the record," he said evenly, "when I say it, I mean the whole package. Everything you are." He gave her time to think about it. "Now, tell me why you love me."

She scowled at him. He was going too fast again. "Who said I loved you?"

"You did. When you went to bed with me."

He looked like a cat with tail feathers around his mouth, she thought wryly. Still miffed about the knife he'd pulled from out of nowhere, she wasn't ready to make things too easy for him. "Why do *you* think I love you?"

"Because I'm great in bed," he said promptly.

Kerry's hazel eyes laughed at him, and he felt something ease in his chest. It was going to be okay. Hell, it was going to be wonderful. She hadn't said it yet, but he liked the idea that the words didn't come easily.

"There is that, but you're also weird," she reminded him.

He nodded. "And bizarre." He scooped her up in his lap, hurting with the need to hold her. "But you're going to marry me, anyway." He felt the jolt and knew she was going to be contrary.

"Maybe," she said carelessly.

"No maybe about it. You're going to marry me. Because you love me. Right?"

He felt it first, the warmth that invaded him and held his heart gently in two small hands. Felt it a beat before Kerry slid her arms around his neck, shivering when his heart thudded against hers.

"Oh, yes," she said softly. "You are my one and only love, forever and ever."

Devin stood up, taking her with him, ignoring her yelp of surprise. He turned around and said, "Get the door." When it slammed behind them, their voices drifted back as he carried her down the hall.

"Did you say forever?"

"And ever," she agreed.

"Kerry?"

"Hmm?"

"Does that make us soulmates?"

Epilogue

Uncle Loe performed two ceremonies that balmy day in June. In the morning, with both families attending, he married Kerry and Devin in the garden. In the afternoon, the yard overflowing with the rest of the guests, he conducted the blessing.

"Well, Mrs. Murphy, what do you think?"

Kerry linked her fingers with her husband's and grinned. "I think I'm married."

"You bet you are. When Uncle Loe ties the knot, it never comes undone." He looked down at Kerry in her simple white dress of fine cotton and wondered how soon the crowd would leave. Not soon enough. Touching the flower in her hair, he said, "It's quite a shindig, isn't it?"

Kerry gazed across the yard, wondering if the earlier owners had used the banyan tree as a canopy for their parties. The tables were draped with pink linen, each bearing centerpieces of candles and containers of floating flowers. Dwayne and his crew had dutifully set up over four hundred chairs for the crowd.

"It's just the way I imagined it would be—beautiful." The house was finished and it was a celebration of the past and present. It had a welcoming warmth, and she was sure it would be exactly what Uncle Loe had predicted—a refuge.

"Luke gave me our wedding present a while ago," Devin said, holding her hand. He wanted to feel the rush of joy that would be shooting through her.

Kerry looked up with a slight frown. "Another one? They already gave us a beautiful set of silver."

Devin grinned. "He said this one was a bribe. It's the deed to the adjoining property—a couple of acres—so we could build a house and you'll be close enough to keep this place running. If that's what you want, we can keep living in the upstairs suite until it's done."

He had been right. Her joy was his now, even though she was trying to be practical.

"Devin! That property is worth a fortune!"

He gave a careless shrug. "He won't even miss it. Besides, he figures you're worth it. What kind of house do you want? Something big and sprawling like this one, I hope. We're going to need room for kids."

He looked into hazel eyes full of love and dreams, and he couldn't resist the temptation. He scooped Kerry up in his arms and spun her around until they were both dizzy.

Life was good, he reflected, overwhelmed by the love radiating from her.

Life was damn good.

* * * * *

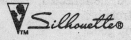